MIRROR OF DREAMS

White Dove Romances

9607

MIRROR OF DREAMS

YVONNE LEHMAN

BETHANY HOUSE PUBLISHERS
MINNEAPOLIS, MINNESOTA 55438

Mirror of Dreams
Copyright © 1996
Yvonne Lehman

Cover design by Peter Glöege

Scripture quotations are taken from the King James Version.

Published by Bethany House Publishers
A Ministry of Bethany Fellowship, Inc.
11300 Hampshire Avenue South
Minneapolis, Minnesota 55438

Printed in the United States of America.

Library of Congress Cataloging-in-Publication Data

Lehman, Yvonne.
    Mirror of dreams / Yvonne Lehman.
      p.   cm. — (White dove romances ; 3)
    Summary: Seriously injured when she is hit by the car driven
by an intoxicated Zac Lambert, Katlyn Chander, embittered
and angry, refuses to forgive him and goes along with her
father's insistence that Zac be severely punished.
    ISBN 1-55661-707-0 (pbk.)
    [1. Alcoholism—Fiction. 2. Family problems—Fiction.
3. Conduct of life—Fiction. 4. Christian life—Fiction.]
I. Title. II. Series: Lehman, Yvonne.
White dove romances ; 3.
PZ7.L5322Mi   1996
[Fic]—dc20   96-25291
                                              CIP
                                              AC

To Lori—
for her suggestions and invaluable critique

and to David—
for police procedural information

and to Kellie—
for her insight

and to Howard—
for always being there

and to Cindy and Lisa—
for medical advice

and to Kathy—
for information about drugs

and to Kati—
for physical therapy techniques

YVONNE LEHMAN is the award-winning author of thirteen published novels, including seven inspirational romances, two contemporary novels, a biblical novel, *In Shady Groves*, and three young adult novels. She and her husband, Howard, have four grown children and five grandchildren, and they make their home in the mountains of North Carolina.

One

"You're *ugly*!" Katlyn Chander shrieked at her reflection in the hand mirror. "Ugly . . . ugly . . . ugly! Sixteen years old . . . and your life is over!"

She slung the mirror across the hospital room. It hit the door with a resounding bang and crashed to the floor, shattering glass all over the tile.

A flash of recollection blasted through her memory. That horrifying instant just before Zac Lambert's fire-engine red car speared her in its headlights, then smashed into the supermarket window, pinning her legs to the storefront. The rest of the evening was a merciful blur, but she didn't need a mirror to tell her how awful she looked as a result.

Her long, black hair had been cut away in at least two places so the doctors could sew up deep gashes. The black circles under her green eyes looked more like misplaced eyebrows. And her face was tatooed with scratches and lacerations. Her bruised body, now lined with red sutures, was limp as a rag doll. Every muscle screamed. Even her bones were sore—those that weren't broken, that is!

Her gaze moved to her legs, crushed below the

7

knees and now encased in plaster splints and covered with a light dressing. Casts couldn't be put on yet because of swelling and possible infection.

No doubt there would be plenty of scars after she healed, too. She could just *see* herself in shorts—not to mention bathing suits!

She groaned. "I'll never be pretty again."

As if to confirm that fact, a smiling face peered around the door. Katlyn didn't feel like smiling back.

Without waiting for an invitation, a woman stepped gingerly inside and picked a path across the debris.

Must be another specialist, Katlyn figured. At least this one was good-looking and wasn't wearing a wrinkled smock with a stethoscope draped around her neck. Instead, she was dressed in a stylish cream-colored suit, and her dark hair was pulled back in a French twist. She'd used a coral gloss on her lips, just a touch of taupe eyeshadow, and blush on her high cheekbones. Whoever she was, she knew her makeup. In fact, Katlyn wouldn't mind looking something like that when *she* was older.

Fat chance of that, Katlyn fumed in the next breath. On second thought, if they ever let her out of this bed, she'd probably look about as awkward as this woman did right now, high-stepping over the splintered glass.

"What happened here?"

Since it was a dumb question, Katlyn wasn't going to answer, then changed her mind. "My mirror slipped out of my hand," she grunted.

"That's seven years bad luck, you know."

"Only seven years?"

"Oh, a few months isn't a lifetime. Before you

know it, you'll be up and around again."

"Yeah. I can hear it now. 'And here's Katlyn Chander, modeling the latest fashions—for the wheelchair set!' " She pushed herself up on her elbows, trying for a more comfortable position.

The woman approached the end of the bed, where some kind of contraption had been rigged up to keep Katlyn's legs elevated. "Is modeling so important to you?"

Katlyn was furious. Easy for *her* to say, standing on two good legs, looking cool and collected. It wasn't *her* life, *her* career on the line. "Are you a doctor?"

"A psychologist. Dr. Lorna Nolan."

"Ohhh, wouldn't you know it?" Katlyn moaned and settled back against the pillow propped behind her head. "They've picked glass out of my face, my head, and my body. Now, they've sent someone to pick my brain!"

The woman laughed pleasantly and walked over to the dresser that had been strategically placed so Katlyn couldn't see herself in the mirror. She'd convinced her mom to bring her hand mirror and makeup case. But that was yesterday, when Katlyn had been really out of it and hadn't much cared *how* she looked. In fact, she'd even fallen for that old line about being "lucky to be alive." But now that she was feeling a little better, she was wondering what was so lucky about it!

"You must have a lot of friends," Dr. Nolan said, glancing around the room at the baskets and vases covering every available surface.

Katlyn shrugged. She hadn't bothered to read the tags to see who had sent them. "Actually, that odor makes me sick. It smells like a funeral around here."

"Maybe you could give some away. There are a lot of people here in the hospital who don't have any flowers."

"And that's supposed to make me feel better?"

"Just making conversation," Dr. Nolan said pleasantly.

Katlyn closed her eyes. No doubt, her daddy was paying a lot for this little "conversation"!

"Oh, what a darling card."

Katlyn cracked an eyelid. She hadn't felt like looking at her cards yet either. *Get well soon! What a crock!* Her mom had displayed them on the dresser so visitors could see them. But so far, she'd managed to avoid visitors, too.

Lorna Nolan brought one card over. "Someone spent some time on this one. Looks handmade."

Reluctantly, Katlyn took the card. Made of construction paper, the design was cut in the shape of a girl with long hair, dressed in a flared A-line skirt. It appeared to have been colored by a young child. Seeing other cutouts behind, folded accordion-style, Katlyn unfolded them. All the little girls were holding hands, like a ring of paper dolls. Each one was different—hairstyle, eye color, dress. On the bottom of each skirt was a name printed in a childish scrawl: *Jenna, Suzie, Erin, Ellen, Molly. . . .*

"Cute idea," Katlyn admitted with grudging admiration. "I wonder who thought of this."

Separate from the others was a slightly larger figure, more artistically rendered. There was no name on the front, but when Katlyn turned it over, she read:

This is our circle of prayer. We pray for you every morning.
It was signed, *Sunshine Daycare and Rose.*

Katlyn scowled. "Rose Ainsworth!" She handed the unusual card back to the doctor, who began to re-fold the images back to back.

"You know her?"

"Oh, not personally. But I know who it's got to be. She's probably Natalie Ainsworth's little sister. There's a whole *litter* of Ainsworth girls."

Dr. Nolan quirked her lip. "Natalie is a friend of yours?"

"Friend?" Katlyn scoffed. "Far from it." The thought gave her a headache, and she rested her head back against the pillow. She'd been told not to get up-set. But nobody had told her how! Seething with re-sentment, she glared at the doctor. "Natalie stole Scott Lambert right out from under my nose. Scott is the brother of *Zac* Lambert—the guy who ran into me!"

"Oh," Lorna Nolan said, nodding. "So that's it." She pulled up a chair, sat down, and leaned forward as if eager to hear more. "It's this Natalie who upsets you."

Somehow, Katlyn found herself opening up. "Well . . . if it wasn't for her, none of this would have hap-pened."

"Oh?"

Katlyn looked down at the wrinkled hospital gown and absently ran a finger over a scratch on her hand. She didn't want to look at the doctor just then. "That's sort of an exaggeration," she admitted. "But . . . she was at this party with Scott, and then they were both in the car with Zac when he lost control of it."

"So you blame *her*?"

"I . . . I don't know all the details yet." Katlyn looked up into the interested gaze of Lorna Nolan. "Daddy says they're all at fault. That Scott and Natalie shouldn't have let Zac drive when he was drunk. He's blaming the entire Lambert family. But it was *Zac* who did it. And he's the one who's going to pay!" Katlyn bit out, her eyes blazing. "My daddy will make sure of that!"

Katlyn's dad, flanked by her mom and twenty-one-year-old sister, Jennifer, stormed through the door just moments after Dr. Nolan left. "We've got to get to the bottom of this. What really happened that night, Princess?"

"Oh, Chan." Her mom put a restraining hand on his arm. "Don't you think it's too early—"

He brushed off her concern. "She's going to have to talk about it sooner or later, Gina. Conferences with our attorney . . . testimony in court . . ."

Katlyn hated when her parents did that—talked about her like she wasn't even there. "It's okay, it's okay." The psychologist had said it would be better to face the truth. Well, maybe she was right. But right now her dad looked like a smaller version of the tornado that had touched down last spring in Garden City.

Pacing the room, he turned to face her sister. "I need to know one thing, Jennifer. Why didn't you tell Zac to leave when he showed up drunk at the house?"

"I didn't know he was drunk, Dad." Katlyn watched Jen dart her an anxious glance, then looked down at her own hands, entwined in her lap on the sheet.

"Boy, if this doesn't beat all," he ground out, shaking his head. "A little ironic, wouldn't you say, that your mother and I were out with the Lamberts the night of the accident, talking about Helen Lambert's alcohol problem . . . offering to stand by to *help*. . . ."—Katlyn had never seen her dad this mad. The sarcasm was practically *dripping*—"while at that very moment, *her* son was getting into *her* stashed supply of booze and ruining *my* daughter's life!"

"Chan, her life's not ruined," Gina said nervously, her big brown eyes—enormous now—flicking from Katlyn to her husband.

"Well, I don't know what you'd call it!" he roared. "She may never walk again!"

Katlyn felt the wind whoosh out of her chest with as much force as Zac's car had slammed her against the window of the supermarket. So far, no one had let her in on *that* possibility. *Never walk again?*

Two

With the hearing looming before him in a month, Zac Lambert spent most of the first week after the accident holed up in his bedroom overlooking the lake. "I've got to face up to this like a man," he kept telling himself. At nineteen, he should have had the world by the tail. He was a premed student just finishing his sophomore year in college, drove a red Corvette, dated terrific-looking girls, and had never been arrested—

Until last Friday night. But Zac didn't need bars to feel like he was already in prison. He'd almost *killed* a girl! At least, he'd hurt her so badly she might never walk again. And even if not, he didn't deserve to walk either, did he? The Chanders sure didn't think so. And after the press got through with him, he'd probably never be able to face *anyone* again!

Son of Socialite Injures Pedestrian! the headlines had screamed. And if that wasn't bad enough, the story went on to spell it out: *Zachary T. Lambert, son of prominent physician Dr. Lawrence Lambert, seriously injured a sixteen-year-old resident of Garden City—Katlyn Chander—late Friday night when the car he was driving jumped the curb in front of Oakwood Supermarket. Young Lambert had been drinking and . . .*

Zac moaned inwardly. *That blows my shot at med school . . . or anything else, for that matter. I won't be going anywhere . . . except maybe to jail. . . .*

Not even the peaceful view of the lake did much to calm his thoughts, churning like an eggbeater. Dawn at Lake Oakwood, where his family spent a lot of time at his aunt's summer home, was usually pretty awesome—all pink- and gold-streaked sky, mirrored in the blue water. But today—one week after the accident—he saw nothing of the break of day . . . only the breaking of glass as he rammed the Corvette into the storefront, sending the Chander girl straight through the plate-glass window.

Hands laced behind his head on the pillow, Zac stared up at the ceiling. All week he'd refused to speak to anyone except his father—and then only to ask about Katlyn, who was still in the hospital in the little town of Lake Oakwood about an hour's drive from Garden City. "She's in pretty bad shape, son" was all his dad would say. Man! Zac had thought she was off the critical list. Maybe she could *still* die!

Pushing aside the gruesome possibility, Zac forced himself to think of something else. What was he going to do with himself while he waited to find out about Katlyn? Mentally he ticked off his options: Not only had his car been wrecked, his driver's license had been revoked, too. No car or license meant he couldn't work this summer—although he'd probably still be able to mow lawns with the Tornado Relief team that had been set up after the storm. But not even the church youth group would want a drunk driver manning a power mower!

Besides, he'd really had his heart set on doing some volunteer work at the hospital this summer. Make a few brownie points with the medical personnel where his dad worked. When *Zac* was a big-time doctor, he'd need all the contacts he could get.

But who was he kidding? Just like that video game where you try to shoot down a flock of wild geese before they fly offscreen, Zac saw his dreams explode, one by one, and fall apart.

In spite of all he could do, his mind kept replaying that awful night. He clearly remembered driving Scott; Scott's date, Natalie Ainsworth, who'd also been a guest at Aunt Martha's lake house for the Fourth-of-July weekend; and his cousin Cissy to Jennifer and Katlyn Chander's get-acquainted bash. The party was pretty low-key in the beginning—hot dogs, cola, chips, music—that sort of thing.

Then sometime after supper, things began to pick up. Of course, Scott and Natalie, along with the rest of the younger kids, stuck to the soft drinks. And Cissy didn't like the taste of alcohol. Besides, being a model and an actress, she was always watching her weight and checking out her complexion. But the older guys—and some of the girls, too—slipped stuff from the bar into their colas.

The next thing Zac knew, he was getting really ticked off—maybe a little bombed. Scott and Natalie had been wearing those White Dove T-shirts with a Scripture verse printed on the back. White Dove was some kind of purity campaign put on by the youth group at Natalie's church. But that kind of in-your-face Christianity really bugged Zac. And when the booze ran out, he was glad for a chance to skip the party and go buy more. That is, until Scott and Natalie tried to stop him. That's why they'd ended up in his car the night—

He shook off the memory, swung out of bed, and loped over to the window, where he could look out. The dew was still sparkling on the grass, and the slant of the sun rising over the lake sent a dazzling beam into his face that almost blinded him. If he'd been on better terms with God, he'd have to wonder if this was some kind of heavenly sign. Like maybe God was trying to get his attention or something. But it had been so long since Zac had thought of spiritual things or been to church—at least on a regular basis—that he was pretty sure it didn't mean anything. Oh, sure, he was sorry about the accident. He was even sorry he'd been stupid enough to drink too much that night. But he could usually hold a few beers without any trouble. The stronger stuff, too.

His head swam dizzily. What was so wrong with drinking anyway? Most grown-ups he knew drank socially—well, almost everyone . . . except, of course, Aunt Martha. Martha Bryson was what was known as a "pillar of the church." Too bad his mom hadn't followed her big sister's example. Mom . . . her alcoholism had driven his dad away—at least emotionally—and Zac and his brother had had to make out the best way they could . . . with a falling-down drunk mother who embarrassed the daylights out of them in front of their friends.

Right on cue, he could hear her now, calling from outside the door. "Zac? Zac, honey? Are you coming down for breakfast?"

Crossing to the bed again, he flopped down, face

first, and moaned into the pillow. Didn't she know he wanted to be alone? Maybe she'd go away if he didn't answer. Maybe she'd just bring a tray and leave it outside his door, like every other morning.

But what was the use? He'd have to face his family sometime. He couldn't stay in his room forever. Hadn't he better enjoy what little freedom he had . . . while he could?

This morning, he surprised even himself when he called back, "Be there in a minute."

"Oh." His mom hesitated. "We'll wait for you."

He shuffled into the bathroom and stared into the mirror, not wanting to look himself in the eye. Rubbing one hand over his bristly face with its week's growth of beard, he decided not to shave. It'd just give him something else to hide behind.

After a quick shower—still trying to scrub off the slime of the drunk tank—he ran a comb through his dark curls. For a second, he dared to look into the blue eyes, as stormy as the day of the tornado. They seemed to be accusing him, condemning him. . . . He couldn't leave the bathroom fast enough.

It took everything he had just to walk into the breakfast nook, where his family was waiting for him. There they were—dear old Dad . . . his alcoholic mom . . . and Scott—looking like a bunch of vultures. Oh, they'd promised to stand by him through this thing, but why now? They'd never been around before when he needed them! At least his mom hadn't.

She saw him first and jumped up. "Zac! Breakfast is getting cold. Sit down, baby."

Baby! A lifetime ago, it seemed, when he was just

a little guy, his mother had said her boys would always be her babies—no matter how old they got. For a moment there, he really wanted to believe that. Wanted to climb up in her lap and have her tell him everything would be all right. . . .

"Good morning, son," his dad greeted him solemnly as Helen poured him a tall glass of orange juice.

"Hey, welcome back, buddy." That was Scott, the one who never disappointed their parents—at least, not since he'd met Natalie Ainsworth and gotten involved in that White Dove stuff.

Zac mumbled a reply and dropped into the nearest chair.

Lawrence cleared his throat. "Well, I suppose this calls for a celebration," he said with a little too much enthusiasm to be real, Zac thought. "Shall we . . . pray?"

Since when had the busy Dr. Lambert slowed down long enough to pray over a meal unless Aunt Martha was around? Glancing about, Zac noticed that she wasn't. Neither were Natalie and Cissy. They'd probably gone back to Garden City to give the family time to sort things out.

"Heavenly Father," Lawrence began hesitantly, "we appreciate this food that sustains our bodies. We . . . need your strength even more . . . for what's ahead of us. Help us . . . please." He came to an uncertain halt, then mumbled a hasty "Amen."

"Would someone pass Zac the eggs?" Helen spoke up brightly. "They're sunny-side up—just the way you like them, honey."

Zac wasn't hungry, but he went through the motions. As the bowl was passed, he spooned some onto his plate.

Even the eggs with their bright yellow centers seemed to be mocking him. The first bite tasted like sawdust.

Small talk swirled about him, bouncing off. Just a bunch of idle chitchat. He finally interrupted with the question that had been gnawing on him all week. "Uh . . . what's the maximum sentence I can get, Dad?"

Pausing in the act of spearing a slab of ham, fork in midair, his dad eyed Zac soberly and his face drained of color. "Maximum?" he echoed. "Well, it depends on the Chander girl's condition at the time. But my attorney says . . . a $1,000 fine and 364 days in jail—and then . . . there's the possibility of civil liability."

Zac felt like a wad of cotton was permanently lodged in his throat. He could have a police record. He'd be a man without a future—without a chance of getting into medical school.

He bolted out the back door and stood on the patio, gulping in the fresh air. But it didn't help. Nothing helped! *God, why did you let this happen?* he called out silently, not surprised when there was no answer from the placid blue sky. He didn't deserve an answer.

"Zac?" His dad's voice came from behind him. Then he was caught up in a giant bear hug, both men leaning into each other. Zac gave it up then and let the heaving sobs come. For several minutes, he stood there, blubbering like a baby.

"Son, I know I've let you guys down. Haven't been around enough. And with your mother's problem . . . well, she's promised to get help. And we're both going to be here for you from now on."

Man, did that sound good! Zac was almost tempted to believe it. But he'd fallen for that kind of thing before, and it never lasted. His mother was an alcoholic—no matter how many new leaves she turned over. And once an alcoholic, always an alcoholic. Right now, he needed someone he could depend on.

Zac moved away, swiping at his eyes, feeling really weird that his dad had seen him cry. "Well, thanks a lot, Dad, but I'm guilty, you know. There were eye-witnesses, a breathalyzer test, the whole nine yards. I don't stand a chance. I'm dead meat."

Zac watched as his dad, hands in his pockets, moved to the edge of the patio and gazed out over the still water. Funny that Zac had never noticed how gray his dad's hair was getting at the temples. . . .

Neither of them spoke until Lawrence broke the silence. "It's true that the Chander girl is in serious trouble. But it's also true that medical science can work wonders these days. . . ." His voice trailed off as he continued to stare at the horizon. "And there's Someone who knows *more* than doctors. Someone who can help us . . . if we let Him."

He turned to face Zac. "Son, I think it's about time you and I got to know Him a little better."

Zac flushed and ducked his head. "But the damage is done, Dad. I did it. I hurt Katlyn. Even *God* can't change that."

There was another long silence. "The verdict isn't in yet, son. We don't have all the lab reports on the Chander case. The hearing hasn't been held. Maybe that's what faith is all about, Zac. Believing that the best can come out of the worst. . . ."

Maybe. But Zac wasn't convinced. It was going to be a long summer—a very long summer.

Three

"Zac wants to apologize to you . . . about the accident . . . in person, Natalie," Scott mumbled around a nail he was holding between his teeth. He got in another few licks with the hammer before turning to see how she was taking the idea.

Bending over the sawhorse where she was cutting a two-by-four to replace some damaged boards on the old Johnson place, Natalie swiveled her head to stare at him. She'd been really surprised when Scott had decided to come home to Garden City—with Katlyn still in the hospital at Lake Oakwood. But he'd explained that there wasn't anything he could do for her right now. Besides, he'd promised to help out with the youth group project.

"Your brother doesn't have to see me," Natalie said. "He's got plenty on his mind without worrying about that. Besides, I wasn't hurt. Just a little shaken up is all."

Scott reached for another handful of nails, looking grim. "I wouldn't blame you if you didn't want to have anything to do with *any* of our family again."

"Come on, that's not what I meant." Natalie straightened, rubbing out the kinks in her back. "We've already been through all that. It's not *your* fault

Zac got drunk that night . . . or that your mom has—*had*"—she corrected herself—"a drinking problem. I really think it's great she's trying now."

"Yeah." Scott picked up the piece of fiberboard Natalie had just cut, and drove a nail through the flimsy wood—so hard she was afraid it would shatter. She found another hammer and moved over to help him.

"At least I *hope* Mom's going to go through with it this time," he went on. "She's promised to go back to Alcoholics Anonymous and even MADD—you know, Mothers Against Drunk Driving—but . . . we'll see."

They worked on in silence for a few minutes before Scott spoke again. "Nat . . . I'm sorry about last week. I'd wanted you to have a good time."

Natalie's heart did a flip. Hammer in hand, she paused. Better not do any nailing right now. She'd be sure to miss and end up with a mushroom for a thumb! "I had a great time, Scott—before the accident anyway."

He glanced over at her, his warm brown eyes looking like melted chocolate. "You're a terrific girl. I really like being with you."

Was she hearing things, or had Scott Lambert just said what she *thought* he said? Flustered, she dropped a nail. "Oops!"

As she bent to retrieve it, Scott reached for it, too, and in the process, their heads collided.

"Oof!"

"Ouch!"

They straightened, then looked at each other and laughed kind of nervously. "I think we've been out in the sun too long," Scott joked. "Time out—before there's *another* accident!"

"Come to think of it, you probably shouldn't be out-side doing all this hard work so soon." Natalie threw him a concerned glance. "How's your head—not the bump I just gave you, but the cut you got last Friday night?"

He touched the bandaged spot on his forehead, al-most covered by a shock of thick wavy hair. "It's better. My dad's a doctor, remember, and he wouldn't let me take any chances. Besides, I'd rather be here right now."

Sweaty and red-faced, as much from embarrass-ment as from the heat, they headed for a big oak tree in the side yard, where jugs of water and cups had been set out for the workers. Several of their friends were there ahead of them—sprawled out in the shade or swigging down the cold water.

Stick Gordon, who had been painting the front porch, had a big smear of white paint on his cheek. Na-talie had to smile. The standard line around school was that the tall, lanky guy—whose close-cropped hair re-sembled a paintbrush—could paint with*out* a brush . . . if he used his head! But today he wasn't his usual goofy self.

Even Ruthie, Natalie's best friend in the whole world, looked sober-faced. The feisty redhead, with a personality to match, was always good for a laugh. But not today. The whole crowd was moving like a bunch of zombies, Natalie thought. Nobody wanted to men-tion what was on everyone's mind—the accident and Katlyn Chander!

Natalie poured two cups of water and handed one to Scott, who popped a couple of aspirin into his mouth and tossed them down. Then she plopped be-side him under the shade of a maple tree.

"Nat, there's a favor I'd like to ask you. Uh . . . someplace I'd like to take you," Scott began.

Natalie felt her heart jump right into her throat. Could he be asking for another date? *Come on, Nat. Don't go jumping to conclusions. Katlyn needs him now.*

"I'd like to get back out to Lake Oakwood this weekend to see how Katlyn's doing. But before that . . . there's Zac." Scott circled the rim of his cup with one finger. "He's decided to rejoin the human race . . . at least, until the trial. And since the Chanders won't have anything to do with him, he really does want to square things with *you*. He hasn't gone out yet. It's pretty tough facing everyone after . . . well, you know. So . . . it'd be a lot easier if I could take *you* to *him*."

Natalie felt her spirits plunge clear to the pit of her stomach. *Told you so!* she told herself. *Scott may enjoy 'being around you,' but it's Katlyn he really likes!* Then in the next breath, she was mentally kicking herself. *How can you be so selfish? Katlyn's in trouble, and all you can think about is if Scott's going to ask you out again!*

Squaring her shoulders, Natalie put the thought out of her mind. "Sure, Scott. I'll go see him. When did you have in mind?"

With youth directors Andy and Stephanie Kelly called out of town suddenly for a funeral in Andy's family, the project was put on hold for the rest of the week. And on Thursday afternoon, Natalie was seated in Scott's cranberry sports car, heading toward his home in Garden Acres.

"Thought you ought to know, Nat. Zac asked Cissy

to come, too," Scott explained on the way over.

"Fine with me." Natalie really liked Scott's cousin Cissy Stiles, the girl who had everything and was the envy of Shawnee High. But Natalie hadn't gotten to know the real Cissy until the night of the tornado. That's when Natalie had found out how empty life was for the older girl. Who'd have believed they'd end up good friends?

But what in the world could any of them say to help Zac? He was definitely guilty. Natalie had been sitting in the backseat of the car when he'd run Katlyn down. *All we can do is pray*, she thought as Scott turned into the long drive leading to the elegant Georgian mansion where he lived in the ritziest section of town.

Natalie had been impressed the first day she'd seen it. Her whole house would fit into the spacious living room and foyer. But all that money and social prominence hadn't kept Scott's mother from becoming an alcoholic . . . or Zac from facing jail! Now, as Scott pulled up in front of the house, Natalie noticed that Zac's Corvette was missing from its usual spot. She wondered how long it would be before he could drive it again.

Cissy and Zac were sitting on the patio around the pool when Scott and Natalie walked up.

"Hi, Nat," Cissy said, brightening a little at the sight of them.

The older girl looked cool and gorgeous, Natalie thought, in light blue shorts and a tank top that matched her eyes, and her blond hair caught the sunlight as she stood up to give them each a hug. But she was quick to move back into the shade after the greeting. Wouldn't do for a model to get an uneven tan, she'd told Natalie before.

"I can't believe you came, Natalie," Zac spoke up.

She'd never seen Scott's older brother like this. She remembered how disgusted she'd been the night of the wreck and how she and Scott had tried to keep Zac from driving in his intoxicated state. But this wasn't the same guy. This one was cold sober . . . and pretty pathetic. He didn't even appear to be as tall as he had the first time she'd met him—like he'd shrunk or something. And before, he'd been so outgoing and friendly. Today, he acted downright shy and fumbled for words.

"I . . . I want to . . . uh . . . thank you all for coming," he began. "This isn't easy, but I've got to do it . . . face-to-face."

He motioned Natalie toward a lounge chair near Cissy, while Scott perched on one end of the diving board. From here, rays of sunlight bounced off the water like falling stars. But Zac didn't have his mind on the scenery.

"I guess Scott told you why I wanted to see you."

Natalie nodded. "You don't have to do this, Zac."

"Yes, I do." He hung his head. "I'm a criminal and a drunk. And you could have been hurt or killed that night. You could have ended up like . . ." His voice broke and trailed off.

"But I *wasn't*," she reminded him. "Besides, there's a whole lot more to you than what happened that night."

"Not anymore." He shook his head. "All I've got ahead of me now is a criminal record and jail time. I've shot down every hope and dream I've ever had."

"Oh, I don't know about that," Cissy said. "It

seemed like there was no hope for your mom. But it was the accident that jolted her into realizing what her alcoholism had done to her family. Not only is she going to start attending AA meetings, but she was telling me a little while ago that she'll be helping Natalie's mom at the Sunshine Daycare."

Natalie was startled. Mom hadn't told her that.

"She's going to speak up about her problem instead of trying to hide it," Cissy finished.

Zac nodded. "Guess I never understood her weakness for alcohol until . . . it happened to me."

"Sure, bro," Scott put in. "See? Some good has already come out of this. Maybe you could do the same thing—talk about it and try to help someone else see the light."

Natalie felt awful as Zac's gaze bored into her. What did he expect her to do about it? Then something occurred to her. "As president of our youth group, Zac, I know Andy and Stephanie are always looking for people to give their testimony. Scott did that at the beginning of the summer. I wonder . . . do you suppose— would you be willing to tell *your* story—maybe let the other kids know that drinking doesn't pay? Especially drinking and driving? That it can change someone's life in a matter of seconds?"

Natalie waited while Zac studied the float bobbing on the surface of the pool. She followed the direction of his gaze. That's how life was—up and down, up and down. Right now, Zac was about as down as a person could get.

"I don't know if I'm ready for something like that. I-I'll have to think about it."

"Sure. Take your time. It was just a thought. But just so you'll know—" Natalie turned to the others. "I've already written to Officer Burns, the man working the desk at the police station the night of the accident. I thought it would be good for the group to hear from a policeman who sees this kind of thing a lot and could give us some pointers. But, Zac," she turned to him again, "it's *your* story that would really make a difference."

His expression changed from sad to sullen. "Who cares about *my* story? I know the Chanders don't. They've already tried me, judged me, and hung me out to dry. They won't even take my calls to find out how Katlyn is. If it weren't for my dad . . ."

With that, Zac bolted from his chair and disappeared into the house through the French doors.

"Man! He's in worse shape than I thought," Scott said, looking distressed.

Cissy jumped to her feet and paced the pool area. "There's got to be something we can do—to help Zac . . . and Katlyn, too!"

"I'm not too sure." For once, Natalie couldn't see much hope either. "The Chanders probably blame Scott and me for not taking the keys away from Zac that night."

"I *tried*," Scott put in. "But you know how Zac is— bullheaded and a couple years older—and stronger."

"Well, they surely wouldn't keep *me* from trying to see Katlyn." Cissy paced some more. "After all, we're next-door neighbors and have a lot of the same interests—clothes, makeup . . . you know."

"Actually, if anyone could turn this thing around,

it's Natalie here." Natalie blushed when Scott focused his attention on her.

Cissy stopped her pacing and turned to look at Natalie. "That's right. You helped me the night I was on my way to elope with Ron, remember, Nat? That's when you gave me the little white dove to remind me that God would be with me . . . no matter what. Without it, I don't think I'd have survived the storm—not to mention the heartache when Ron ran off and left me!"

Feeling really uncomfortable, Natalie changed the subject. "Well, *someone* has to get through to Mr. Chander."

Cissy sank into the nearest chair and crossed her slender legs, tapping one sandaled foot on the paved patio. "Where Katlyn is concerned, that man is about as hard as this concrete. I mean, she's Daddy's little darling."

Natalie sat for a minute, thinking. The last thing she wanted to do was throw Scott at Katlyn. But it was pretty clear how he felt about her anyway. Besides, this wasn't the first time she'd suspected that the hand-writing was on the wall: Scott liked Katlyn; Katlyn needed Scott and was crazy about him. So . . .

"I've got an idea," Natalie murmured. Both heads swiveled in her direction. "I think there's only one person who can get through to the Chanders . . . Katlyn, at least. And Katlyn can talk her dad into anything." Cissy and Scott waited to hear what she had to say. "*You're* the one, Scott."

Now that she'd done "the right thing," Natalie waited for the good feeling that usually followed. Nothing. Maybe sometimes it didn't come right away

. . . or maybe—and this was the hardest thought of all—giving Scott up would *never* feel good.

Just about the time Natalie was wishing she'd kept her big mouth shut, Helen and Lawrence Lambert stepped out onto the patio, looking troubled. *What is he doing home this time of day?* Natalie wondered.

Dr. Lambert cleared his throat, glancing around. "Where's Zac? I'm afraid we have some bad news."

"He went inside, Dad," Scott told him. "He's probably in his room. What's up?"

"We just heard that the Chander girl will go back into surgery tomorrow. Complications of compound fractures of the tibia and fibula."

"Wh-what does that mean?" Natalie squeaked.

All eyes were fixed on Dr. Lambert, who proceeded to explain in ordinary language. "Both legs are involved, but it's the left they're concerned about. There's a possibility of damaged nerves. At this point, no one knows the extent of the damage . . . or if she will be left with some residual paralysis."

There was not a sound except for the hum of the water filter in the pool and the chattering of a squirrel scampering across the lawn nearby. Natalie felt as if there wasn't enough air to breathe as everyone waited for Dr. Lambert's next words.

"Her fever should have gone down by now, but it hasn't. Even with an antibiotic regimen, the doctors haven't been able to prevent infection in her left leg. If it isn't brought under control soon . . ."

Natalie barely noticed when Zac stepped through the door just in time to hear his father finish. ". . . the leg may have to be amputated."

Four

Katlyn was worried. Not only was the pain in her left leg getting worse, there was no feeling at all in her left foot! But she *could* feel a definite tension in the atmosphere when an LPN or technician came in to take her temperature or draw blood. It wasn't so much what they were saying; it was the look on their faces that gave them away. And when a nurse hooked her back up to the IV, Katlyn was really scared.

"I thought I was through with all that," she complained.

Katlyn noticed that the nurse wouldn't look her in the eye but kept fiddling with the drip. "Oh, this is just another antibiotic. An extra precaution."

"For what?"

"To make sure your infection clears up."

"*What* infection?"

The nurse got real busy all of a sudden. "Just lie still. I need to take your temp."

Katlyn wasn't fooled. "Okay, tell me what's going on," she demanded. "I have a right to know."

The nurse popped the thermometer into her mouth and felt for a pulse. Muzzled like a rabid dog, Katlyn could do nothing but fume inwardly.

This small-town hospital was beginning to give her the creeps. They should have moved her back to Garden City General where things were bigger and better. Not to mention more up-to-date. This place was positively from the Dark Ages.

The minute the thermometer was out of the way, she spoke up again. "I thought I was going home today."

But the nurse was writing down the numbers on a chart. Then she bustled out almost before Katlyn got the question out of her mouth. Katlyn hadn't a clue as to what was going on here.

Nobody would give her a straight answer. When her parents arrived, all her mother would say was, "Honey, you have a little fever. They need to keep you here long enough to find out what's causing it."

"Well, the sooner, the better," Katlyn griped.

There was no doubt she wasn't getting any better. Her leg was throbbing now, and she had a killer of a headache. When Lorna Nolan dropped by late that afternoon, Katlyn was relieved to see her. Maybe the psychologist would give her some answers.

"Katlyn, we've decided it's time to bring you into the loop," Dr. Nolan began. "You're a big girl, and you can handle . . . whatever comes. But it's only fair you know the possibilities."

By this time, Katlyn's head was pounding like a jackhammer, and she closed her eyes to shut out the light. "Would someone please tell me what I'm supposed to be able to handle?" she muttered.

"Here's Dr. Jordan now. He'll explain everything."

Katlyn opened her eyes and blinked to focus more clearly on the short, balding surgeon, still wearing his green scrubs from a recent surgery. He sure didn't look like one of those hunks on *ER* or *Chicago Hope*. But what could one expect? This wasn't television, and it wasn't Chicago . . . or even Garden City. This was some dinky little hospital in the sticks.

"We don't anticipate the worst," Dr. Jordan began hopefully, "but you do have some infection in your left leg, Katlyn. The stronger antibiotic should bring it under control. And you have youth and good health on your side."

"I've already heard that—several days ago," Katlyn argued. "So why am I not getting any better?"

"Some wounds take a little more time to heal than others. But your right leg is coming along beautifully."

She made a face. "It looks really ugly to me—all red and puffy."

"A little swelling is to be expected, but there's no sign of infection there. Let's just give the left leg a chance to catch up, shall we?"

Katlyn glanced at the people circling her bed—the surgeon, Mom and Dad, the psychologist, even Jennifer . . . and their pastor from the church in Garden City? When had *he* come? And why? Was there something the doctors hadn't told her?

"You're afraid the infection won't clear up," Katlyn guessed. "I could die or . . . lose my leg?"

Horrified, she struggled to push herself into a sitting position, then fell back against the pillow. She couldn't very well sit up with both legs strapped into hammocks!

Suddenly her mother was at her side, holding her hand, stroking her hair. "Calm down, honey. We don't want you worrying."

"Calm down?! How can I calm down?" She looked again at the white faces hovering over her. No one said a word. "It's true, isn't it? I really could lose my leg!" Frantic, she glanced over at her dad. "Daddy? Tell me I'm not going to lose my leg. Tell me it's not going to happen!"

Her father's expression told her everything—but not what she wanted to hear. He shook his head, looking as if he might burst into tears at any moment.

"No!" she burst out. "I'd *die* if I had to look like . . . like *that*!"

Reverend Clark stepped nearer the bed and laid his hand over hers on the sheet. "Katlyn, there's . . . Someone you may have overlooked in all the confusion. God. He's listening. We can still pray."

She swiped at her wet face and looked up at him. "Will you pray that I'll keep my leg?"

He gave a fair imitation of a smile, but she wasn't convinced. "We pray for God's will, Katlyn. That's what we all want."

"But *I* want my leg!" Somewhere in the back of her mind, Katlyn thought maybe she should be asking God to spare her *life*. She closed her eyes, pleading silently.

Reverend Clark knelt beside the bed and prayed for her recovery, for the doctors and nurses who would be taking care of her, for a quick response to the medication. ". . . but thy will be done, Lord. Amen."

Katlyn's eyes flew open. Why had he tacked on that phrase? "Why *wouldn't* God want to heal my leg?"

"God wants all of His children to be strong and healthy."

"Then why aren't we? Why did this happen to me?"

Before the pastor could answer, Katlyn's dad leaned over to speak to her, his nostrils flaring in his red face. His dark eyes seemed to be shooting sparks. "It wasn't *God* who did this to you, Katlyn. Don't blame Him! Put the blame where it belongs." His hands clenched into fists. "On Zac Lambert!"

"Chan," her mother put out a hand, "this isn't the time. . . ."

Suddenly everything was whirling . . . spinning . . . like a child's top . . . or a tornado. . . .

"Give her a sedative," Dr. Jordon said briskly.

Katlyn hardly felt the shot. What was a little sting compared to the possibility of losing her leg?

Reverend Clark slipped out first, then the surgeon and the nurses. Jennifer leaned over and kissed her on the cheek. "I've heard them talking about you, Kat. They don't really think there's any big problem. They're just trying to prepare you for the worst. Now think good thoughts, little sis, and we'll see you tomorrow."

Through a haze, Katlyn noticed that Lorna Nolan had hung back until the others had cleared out. Now the woman was walking around the room, touching cards and flowers, waiting. Waiting . . . for what?

"You think I'm a spoiled brat, don't you?" Katlyn mumbled to her back, definitely feeling the effects of the sedative.

Lorna turned around to face her. "I think you're a spunky young lady who has every right to be bitter.

You've been hurt. You're incapacitated—for the moment. You've lost your freedom. You're angry and scared. But you have a lot of spirit, Katlyn. It will help you recover—if you don't let it eat away at you and make you more bitter."

Spirit! Natalie would say she needed *God's* Spirit. Well, Katlyn wasn't a *heathen*. And she'd already prayed for healing. But she wasn't going to add that frightening phrase about "His will." Still, if God knew *everything*, why would He listen to Katlyn Chander?

She felt herself drifting off. *Guess I'll have to wait for an answer till I wake up. . . .*

Sometime in the night, Katlyn came out of her drugged sleep. She was burning hot! Her fever must be high, but when she asked the nurses *how* high, they wouldn't tell her. Doctors kept appearing to examine her wound. She was given medication but no longer bothered to ask what it was for.

When she flopped her arms and moved her head from side to side, the ever-present nurse cautioned her against moving her legs. So she lay as still as she could, feeling first hot, then cold; dry, then clammy. She hurt all over—her legs, her stomach, her head.

Finally she felt too weak to move at all. But like the fever, a horrible fear tingled through her body: God wasn't going to answer her prayers—or the minister's—or anyone else's. She was going to lose her leg—and God wasn't going to do anything about it.

She moaned. She didn't care when she felt another needle prick her arm. She couldn't hurt any worse.

Then . . . slowly . . . she stopped caring at all. . . .

In her new summer sundress, she felt more beautiful than she'd ever felt in her life. She twirled in front of the mirror, laughing at her reflection. As she spun, her long, black hair, glistening with a blue-black sheen, fanned out from her face in soft ringlets. Shaded by long, dark lashes, her emerald green eyes danced. A slight blush touched her cheeks, and her lips turned up in a satisfied smile. Everything was perfect!

She left her room and sat at the bar in the great room of her parents' lake house. From a darkened corner, Zac appeared, holding a huge goblet of sparkling pink champagne. He looked awesome in a black tux, so handsome he almost took her breath away.

He was smiling as he approached. He offered her the goblet. She took a sip and handed it back to him. His piercing blue eyes seemed to be telling her secrets. She giggled with delight.

He lifted the glass high in a toast—then higher and higher. Still smiling, he tipped the goblet.

What was he doing?

Zac's eyes took on a wild look, and his smile became a grotesque grimace. He threw back his head and began to laugh.

Looking up, she saw the liquid tilting toward the rim of the glass. "Please, Zac, no!"

But he didn't listen. As if in slow motion, the drops began to fall—like pink rain. She wanted to hide her face in her hands. But she couldn't move, couldn't look away. The champagne splashed onto her hair, her hands, her face. . . .

She looked down. Her hair hung around her face in limp strings. Her beautiful new dress was drenched. She *watched in horror as the pink stain turned red—fire-engine red—like blood. She screamed, but no sound came out of her mouth.*

The bloodred champagne kept coming, flowing over her body. Zac was laughing like a maniac now. She was paralyzed with fear.

The liquid grew sticky and warm, clinging to her skin like hot glue. It dripped in globs onto the floor until the whole room was slick and slimy. She could feel the murky goo rising higher, seeping through her sandals, oozing between her toes, covering her ankles, her knees. . . .

When the stuff was waist deep, Zac turned and walked away, disappearing into the darkness, his evil laughter trailing over his shoulder.

Katlyn slipped from the barstool. She would swim out of here. But when she tried to stand, she found she had no legs! She was sinking into the thick blood . . . being sucked under like quicksand. She choked as it filled her mouth, her throat, her lungs. She couldn't breathe. . . .

"Katlyn!"

"Katlyn! Katlyn!"

Someone . . . somewhere was calling her name . . . bringing her back from the terrible darkness.

"Katlyn, wake up," the voice insisted. "We're right here to help you."

Someone lifted her out of the slimy mire. Katlyn was trembling all over, soaked in sweat, and her breath was coming in shallow gasps.

"Breathe deeply now. You were only dreaming."

She tried . . . strangled . . . coughed.

Finally she opened her eyes, squinting to see who

had saved her. All she could make out was a white blur. Had she been having a nightmare—or was it some inner knowing?

She clamped her eyes shut, not daring to look and see if she still had two legs—or only one!

"What am I doing here?" Zac muttered to himself as he ambled into the foyer of Garden City General Hospital, hands stuffed into the pockets of his jeans.

He answered his own question. "Because you'd lose your mind if you did nothing until the trial but vege out in front of the TV—*that's* what you're doing here." It hadn't taken much for his dad to talk him into coming along while he made hospital rounds.

Since his father was seeing patients on the maternity floor, Zac decided to check out the Rehab Center, located in a separate wing on the ground level. It was a brand-new facility, praised in the newspaper for its "state-of-the-art technology and innovative therapies for patients recovering from everything from sports injuries to cancer surgery." Even with all his plans for med school down the drain, Zac was fascinated.

Taking the crosswalk to the building, he stepped through the double doors into a reception area that looked like anything *but* a hospital waiting room. Life-sized posters of sports celebrities and other public figures plastered the walls, and comfortable lounge chairs were arranged for easy conversation while families and friends waited for therapy sessions to end. In one corner, darkened for the purpose, a continuous-showing projector had been set up to run footage of actual therapies underway inside. *Neat idea*, Zac thought.

"Lets the patient's family know what's going on here and what can be done at home to supplement our work." A sharp-looking young woman, dressed in an exercise leotard, leggings, and tank top, came around the desk where she had been sitting. Her name tag read *Terri*.

"Do you have a family member in our program— or are you sneaking in to take advantage of our Nautilus equipment?" she teased.

"N-no. That is . . . neither one," Zac stuttered. "I mean, I'm just killing time while my dad—" He skidded to a halt. Maybe he wasn't supposed to be here. If so, he might get his father in trouble. . . .

"Oh, no problem. Just make yourself at home. Or, better still, come with me, if you like, and I'll show you around while there's a lull in the action. Everyone's at lunch right now except me."

Zac followed the woman through a pair of swinging doors into a huge room that resembled a gymnasium— except for the flowers blooming on one wall. The huge blossoms and a few wild animals had been painted in neon colors—by very young artists, Zac figured. It looked something like a jungle—on some other planet—since most of the flowers were bigger than the animals.

Catching his puzzled expression, Terri grinned. "We get a lot of kids. Sooner or later during therapy, they get a chance to make their contribution to our mural. Some are a little more . . . artistic . . . than others.

"The small rooms off to the side"—Terri pointed

toward the cubicles lining two sides of the main room—"are used for individualized treatment—moist heat packs, ultrasound, massage—that sort of thing.

"Out here, of course, is our exercise equipment—Nautilus, Kincom, Biodex—for strengthening muscles and ligaments after surgery or injury. The usual stuff you'd find in a really good fitness center—except better," she said with a twinkle in her eye. "The parallel bars are for patients who, for one reason or another—stroke, accident, cancer surgery—are relearning the use of their limbs. That reminds me. . . ." She glanced at her watch. "I'd better get back to my desk. I have a one o'clock coming—"

A loud noise interrupted her explanation. Zac turned to follow her gaze. Wheeling himself through the extra-wide door was a child of about eight—baseball cap on backward, T-shirt two sizes too big, and a grin splitting his face from ear to ear. "Hey, Miss Terri! I'm here!"

Zac took in the scene—wheelchair and all—then almost gagged. Beneath a pair of grubby cutoffs, one of the boy's legs extended to a foot encased in a tennis shoe. The other—from the knee down—was missing!

Five

He's just a little kid! Zac thought when he saw the little guy in the wheelchair. The next thought sent his spirits plunging to an all-time low. *Wonder if this is what's facing Katlyn Chander?*

"Well, hello, Chad, you're right on time." Terri stepped forward to greet the child just as a crew of technicians—guys and gals in exercise shorts and T-shirts—burst through the doors on the opposite side of the room, probably on their way back from lunch.

"All set for your session with Joel?"

"You bet!"

"Chad Greer, this is . . ." Terri turned to Zac with a puzzled expression on her face. "I don't think you ever mentioned your name."

He stuck out his hand and gripped the little boy's hand. "I'm . . . uh . . . Zac," he introduced himself quickly.

There was a brief flicker in Terri's face—like she might be remembering something—before she turned to Chad again. "Okay, little guy. Here comes Joel now. He'll help you with your prosthesis . . . then we'll see how long it'll be before you qualify for the Olympics.

Special Olympics," Terri explained under her breath as a brawny guy, muscles bulging, approached.

Zac didn't miss the more-than-friendly glance the two exchanged before Joel rolled the child toward one of the small rooms off to the side.

"See ya later, Miss Terri!" Chad called back to her. "I'm going to do great today!"

"What happened to him?" Zac asked, not really wanting to know. What if the little boy had lost his leg in a car accident?

"Cancer. The surgeons think they got it all, but they won't know for a while. In the meantime, there's a lot we can do to give him as normal a life as possible. Hey—" she interrupted herself—"have you had lunch? There's a little snack room in the back if you'd like to grab a sandwich, and I'll tell you more."

Zac was still reeling. He wasn't sure he wanted to know more. But Terri was leading him through the maze of patients and physical therapists already at work on the various pieces of equipment stationed about the room. Wheelchairs and canes lined the walls.

In the snack room, deserted now except for the two of them, several vending machines offered a variety of choices.

"What'll you have—hot dog, ham and cheese, burger? If we nuke them in the microwave, they're almost edible." Terri gave a wry laugh.

Zac wasn't very hungry, but Terri had been really nice to take so much of her time that he didn't feel like refusing. "A burger would be fine."

She put two in the microwave oven while Zac fed a drink machine and extracted a couple of juices.

"I have to tell you that everything here's low fat, and the burgers are made out of soy. They're not too bad. But we stress good dietary habits, so we have to set an example." She gave a tired sigh. "Still, we're always on a tight schedule, so as far as fast foods go, this is the best we can offer."

Zac slathered on a low-fat dressing of some kind, then added a couple of pickles and some lettuce and tomato from the small refrigerator that Terri told him was stocked by volunteers.

As they ate, she talked about Chad. "He's come a long way—he's been fitted for a prosthesis that will enable him to walk again. But he still has a lot of work to do. The muscles above his knee have to be stimulated each session to manage the new limb—not very pleasant, I'm afraid. Then there's gait training—where he actually puts his weight down and begins to take a few steps. In a couple more weeks, he should be ready to walk the distance—that is, to cover the entire length of the mat, holding on to the parallel bars. Then we'll try him in the pool. His wound has healed, so that will provide added exercise for the remaining muscles—and be a lot more fun."

"Where's his family? I noticed he was alone when he wheeled himself in. Or are they waiting outside?"

Terri took a swallow of juice before answering. "That's the saddest part. Chad's from the Projects, an orphan, though he lives with an aunt. She drops him off here on her way to her afternoon work shift, then one of our volunteers takes him home after his session. He has an older brother who's supposed to be looking out for him, but I don't know what kind of an influence the guy is." She frowned. "Sometimes this job gets to me. There are so many people . . . so many problems . . . and not enough of us to go around. You just can't adopt all the needy children in the world. But if Joel and I were already married . . . I'd be tempted."

Oh, so there was *something going on between Terri and Muscleman!* Zac munched on some chips, thinking about what she had just said. He'd never met anyone who cared so much—except maybe Natalie Ainsworth. And *she* wasn't a health professional; she was a do-gooder. Oh, he supposed his dad cared about his patients, but he never talked much about them. Medicine was just a job, Zac figured—a job that paid big bucks.

Terri's next question jolted him out of his thoughts. "I haven't given you a chance to say much of anything. So what are *you* doing to keep busy this summer?"

He choked on a swallow of apple juice, then made a production out of finding a napkin to wipe his mouth. *If she only knew!* But she wouldn't if he could get out of here fast enough. "Oh, nothing much. But I *do* have to meet up with someone here in the hospital. In fact, he's probably wondering where I am right now. So thanks for the tour . . . and . . . uh . . . just thanks a lot."

He was out of there before she could say another word!

With an hour's drive from Lake Oakwood to Garden City, Katlyn was exhausted by the time her dad turned his long, black Cadillac into their winding drive. The grass rolled out like a carpet on either side, and the hedges were neatly clipped. *"Best-looking lawn in the neighborhood,"* he always bragged. *"And it ought to be. I pay an arm and a leg for lawn services,"* he'd groan.

Katlyn winced. She'd never be able to hear that phrase again without thinking how close she'd come to losing her leg.

"Jennifer's been getting ready for days for your homecoming, Katlyn." Her mom smiled back at her.

Her mom looked positively *gorgeous*, her still-dark hair swept up on top of her head to keep cool, her makeup done to perfection. She and her mom usually didn't get along all that well; in fact, her mom drove her *crazy* half the time. Daddy was Katlyn's favorite—and vice versa—just like Jennifer was Mom's favorite. Or at least, Katlyn had always thought so. But today *everyone* looked pretty wonderful.

They had barely come to a stop—as near the front door as possible—when Jennifer came running out, carrying a huge bouquet of pink and purple balloons. "Welcome home, Kat!"

"Hi, Jen. Thanks for the bal—" Whoa! Who was *that*?

Stepping into view from behind Jennifer was a tall, big-boned woman in a nurse's uniform, batting at the balloons while she tried to open the back door for Katlyn. It would have been hilarious if Katlyn had been able to think straight. Who was this strange person? And why was she here?

"This is Miss Birget, honey," her mom explained. "She's a private-duty nurse who'll be here for a while—just to help out."

Poker-faced, the stout woman held the door as Katlyn's father came around to help her out. "Careful of zee legs now."

As if Daddy wouldn't know to be careful! Who did Miss Priss think she was anyway, ordering him around like that?

He lifted Katlyn gently, maneuvering her legs—now in casts—through the door. Then he carried her into the house and up the curving staircase to her peaches-and-cream bedroom, where the housekeeper was turning down the bed, her plump face all smiles.

"Miss Katlyn, it's so nice to have you home again!"

"Thanks, Mrs. Jennings. It's great to be back. I thought I'd never get out of that . . ." Katlyn broke off, spotting a gleaming black-and-silver wheelchair near the bed, and finished on a gasp—"awful place." The chair looked like some monster just waiting to pounce and devour her in a single gulp.

Her dad lowered her onto the bed, and her mom and Jennifer entered the room. "Everything's all here, darling." Mom *never* called her "darling"! "Telephone, intercom, TV remote. . . ."

"Are you hungry, Kat? Do you want anything to eat or drink?" This time it was Jennifer hovering over her.

Katlyn closed her eyes, her head swimming.

"Can't you see she's tired?" her dad spoke up. "She needs rest. Let's get out and leave her alone. Miss Birget will be staying just across the hall, if you need anything, Princess."

"Thanks, Daddy." How did he always know exactly what to say—almost as if he could read her mind? It had always been that way.

"You know the doctors said your friends could visit with you, darling, just as soon as you're ready." Mom added.

"Yeah, little sis, I'd have invited them all over for a big welcome-home bash if you'd been up to it." Jennifer backed away as Miss Birget advanced on her.

"The patient must rest now. No visitors today."

And just who made Miss Bridget—or whatever her name is—queen of the world? Katlyn fumed to herself. But she was secretly relieved when the whole family disappeared through the door, closing it softly behind them.

"Anysing I can do for you, miss?" the woman asked in her heavy accent.

"Just one. Can you help me to the bathroom?"

The next thing she knew, Katlyn was being lifted like a baby and carried into her peach bath. She was beginning to see why Daddy had hired her. The woman was as strong as an ox! *She must work out with massive weights to be able to lift like this!*

But when she settled Katlyn back into bed, Katlyn caught a whiff of perfume. Hmm. There was more to Miss B. than met the eye. "You're not from around here, that's for sure," Katlyn said. "But I don't recognize the accent."

"I am Svedish. Now, if there is nothing else, I vill leave you to rest."

Katlyn nodded. She was too tired to gripe about not seeing her friends. She didn't think she could have handled it today anyway. Tonya, the girl who was with her the night of the accident, wasn't really a friend. Margarita was in Europe for the summer. In fact, almost everyone she hung out with was either out of the country or spending a few weeks at their summer homes. They were all having fun somewhere—everyone but Katlyn. And now there was this Brunhilda, who was going to police Katlyn's every move. Some summer!

She must have dozed off, because she started when she heard a tap at the door. "Hey, little sis, how's it going?" Jennifer eased herself onto the side of the bed.

Katlyn sighed and pulled herself up on the pillows. "Everyone keeps telling me I'm lucky not to have been killed," she said flatly. "But you can't prove it by me."

"Well, I'm glad you weren't, little sis. And you still have your legs."

"So what? What good are they if I can't walk on them?"

"Don't think like that, Kat. You'll get better soon."

"I can't help it, Jen," she moaned. "It scares me. This whole thing scares me—first the infection, then my whole summer shot . . . on top of not knowing if I'll ever walk again—and now the trial. I don't want to go into a courtroom and testify."

"Maybe you won't have to. Zac has admitted he was drunk. And you have plenty of witnesses that he was the one driving—Scott, Natalie, lots of others."

"Yeah, but Dad wants me there. He said seeing me like this will make a bigger impact. He's really set on putting Zac in jail for a long time."

Jennifer didn't say anything for a moment. "That's what you want, too, isn't it, Kat?"

Katlyn fidgeted and dropped her eyes. Jen, five years older, had always been her best friend, someone she could tell everything to—well, almost everything. But Katlyn still wasn't sure how she felt about the accident. The psychologist had said it might take quite a while to sort it all out. She set her jaw stubbornly. "He ought to pay for what he's done."

"I've been doing a lot of thinking, Kat." Jen got up and walked over to the window. "It was *my* fault there was drinking at our party. I allowed it. But I didn't know about Zac's mom's problem or how drinking might affect him." She turned to face Katlyn. "I'm sorry I didn't take better care of you."

"You're not to blame, Jen. It's like Dad said—Zac's responsible for his own actions."

"I know. But if I'd stopped by the store and bought the milk that afternoon like Mom asked me to, then you wouldn't have tagged along with Tonya that night to the grocery store . . . and Zac wouldn't have hurt you. So, where does the blame really lie?"

Her sister looked so miserable Katlyn felt defensive. "It's not your fault, Jen. You couldn't have known Zac was heading to the store, too, that night—and you know it!"

"But maybe . . . maybe I should tell Dad and Mom I knew there was drinking going on. It seems only fair that Zac shouldn't have to take all the blame."

"Don't do that, Jen. Please! It would make me feel a lot worse if Dad and Mom got mad at you. So don't feel guilty. *You* didn't run over me. *Zac* did! Besides, he probably was drinking before he ever got to the party—alcohol from his mom's stash at home."

Jennifer sat down on the bed again. "Mrs. Lambert's trying so hard, Kat. Speaking to groups. Going to meetings. I hate to think our parents will never be friends with them again . . . or with Cissy's parents either. They were really close."

"Maybe after Zac goes to jail and pays for what he's done, they'll be friends again."

Jennifer shook her head. "It'll never be the same. Not the way Dad feels about Zac hurting you."

"Promise me, Jen . . . promise me you won't tell Mom and Dad there was drinking going on at the party . . . that *I* was drinking," Katlyn squeaked.

"Oh, Kat . . . I didn't know. . . ."

"Please, Jen. Don't tell them."

Jennifer gave her a funny look and took a deep breath. "Okay then . . . I promise." She leaned over and hugged Katlyn. "Now I'd better skedaddle out of here before I get in trouble with Miss B. You're supposed to be resting. See ya later, little sis—after your beauty nap." She winked and eased out of the room.

After Jennifer left, Katlyn lay there a long time, staring at the ceiling. After Jennifer's promise, she should be feeling better. But something was crawling around in her insides, like that creeping itch she felt inside her left cast. There was no way to scratch it.

Well, Dr. Nolan had told her the best way to deal with that was to get her mind on other things. She picked up the remote and clicked on the TV.

She really *had* been sleeping this time, Katlyn knew, because when she woke up, she was feeling tons better. She was even glad to see her mother when she came in with a handful of mail.

"This is all the mail you've received since the accident, darling—along with some you haven't seen. I saved them for you. Your daddy and I think it best to avoid all contact with the Lamberts or the Stiles—since they're related—until after the trial. But I knew you'd want to see these. They're from Cissy and Scott."

"Thanks, Mom." She took the envelopes from her mother. "You *do* know Scott tried to save me. He was the one who yanked the wheel out of his brother's hands and tried to steer the car away from the curb— just not fast enough."

"That's what I've heard." Her mom sighed and sat down in a white wicker chair with a floral cushion that matched the balloon shades over the windows. "And I know Scott and Cissy are not responsible for what happened. It's just that your daddy is so *angry*. You're his little angel, you know."

Angel? Oh, brother! Katlyn looked down at the cards in her hands. Where were the ones from Scott? She sifted through them and quickly found what she was looking for. She'd save them for last. "Nothing from Zac, Mom?"

Gina shrugged helplessly. "Well, he called several times . . . and sent flowers and notes. But as hard as it is . . . I had to agree with your father that we shouldn't receive them. I'm sure the Lambert boy is sorry. People generally are when they've done something terrible and are faced with prison. But we have to think of our daughter before our friends. After all, we're going to have to fight them in a court of law."

"Well, I'd like to see Scott and Cissy, at least."

"Honey . . ."

"Please, Mom. Scott's . . . special. And Cissy

knows a lot of makeup tricks that will help me look better." Yuck! She hated to think what she'd look like in the mirror. She hadn't dared take a peek since that day in the hospital when she'd thrown her hand mirror across the room and broken it into a zillion pieces.

Her mother sighed. "Your father is afraid they might talk you into wanting to go easy on Zac."

"No way, Mom. We won't even talk about the case—like the attorney said. Just remind Daddy of that and that Scott got hurt trying to save my life. Zac's the bad guy here, not his brother. Scott's a *hero*, Mom."

Her mother patted her hand. "Okay, baby. I'll try. But you know your daddy. He can be pretty stubborn when he makes up his mind about something—like someone *else* I know." She laughed lightly.

"But you and I can change Daddy's mind, can't we, Mom?"

"Oh, we've been known to—once in a while," she agreed and left the room with a conspiratorial wink.

Out of sheer boredom, Katlyn looked again at her cards. She was surprised to find some from people she didn't even know who wrote that they were praying for her. She was *not* surprised at the ones from Natalie. Every single one of them listed a Scripture verse. *It'll take more than* that *to make me feel better, Natalie Ainsworth! Like staying away from my guy!*

She put the others aside and dug into Cissy's. Cissy told about rehearsals for her part in a play put on by the summer theater group and hoped Katlyn would feel well enough to be there on opening night, sitting in the first row. *I'm playing a Swedish maid*, she wrote, *but the accent is hard to nail. Take care of yourself and feel better soon. Love, Cissy.*

Interesting. She hadn't said a word about her cousin Zac.

Shaking off the thought, Katlyn tore open a card from Scott and was soon giggling. On the inside of the card, he had drawn stick figures of a boy and a girl—the boy, with a bandaged head; the girl, with her legs in giant casts. Ballooning from the drawing was the caption: *One thing we have in common: They've really kept us in stitches!*

Replacing the card, she closed her eyes for a minute. Scott was so gorgeous. Funny too. They really did have a lot in common—money, looks, the right circle of friends. She just *had* to get him to like her before the summer was over. But how was she going to manage that—trussed up like a Thanksgiving turkey?

Opening her eyes again, she looked toward the window facing the Stileses' house. Even with the spacious lawns between them, from here you could see their swimming pool out back. Boy, it was really going to be awkward—living right next door to people you weren't supposed to talk to! Not that she was *that* close to Cissy. The older girl would be a college freshman in the fall. But Katlyn had always secretly admired Cissy Stiles and wished she could be just like her—beautiful, talented, and smart enough to make all her dreams come true.

There was just one thing: All of *Katlyn's* dreams had turned into nightmares!

Six

"Is it ever good to see *you* all in one piece!" Cissy gushed when she came over the next day.

She'd made it past the front guard—Mom, Daddy, and Jennifer—Katlyn thought with satisfaction. Now there was only a scowling Miss Birget to go.

"A few minutes only, you stay," the nurse insisted. "The patient hass been very ill, you know."

Katlyn rolled her eyes. When was the woman ever going to learn her name and stop calling her "the patient"? "I'm fine. Really. I'll call you if I need you . . . Birget."

When the nurse had left—reluctantly—Katlyn turned to Cissy. "She's driving me bananas. But she's okay," she added, thinking how the stout woman had carried her into the bathroom only that morning and helped her shampoo her hair—gently leaning her over the tub and using the shower spray. "Now fill me in on all the gossip."

"I'd rather hear about *you*. I guess you know you scared us all to death when we heard your leg was infected."

"Yeah, I was lucky." Katlyn felt a little guilty. She

probably ought to be saying something like, "Our prayers were answered." But that was *Natalie's* line! "The doctors said my fever was mostly from some summer bug or other."

"Then . . . everything's okay . . . with your legs?"

Katlyn glanced at the casts and grimaced. "We don't know for sure. I can't put any weight on them yet because I might get something like droopy feet."

Cissy laughed. "Foot drop, you mean."

"That's it. I forgot. With your uncle around, you probably know all kinds of medical terms."

"Not really. It's *Zac* who wants to be the doctor." Cissy's blue eyes widened at the accidental mention of his name. And to cover her slip, Katlyn figured, she hurried on. "Foot drop just means that the foot points down when you walk, so that instead of the heel hitting the floor first, the toes do. In other words, you have to lift your foot higher than normal to compensate."

"Cute." Katlyn scrunched up her face. "That's all I need."

"Oh, it can be corrected with therapy," Cissy went on cheerily.

Katlyn wasn't cheered. She was well aware that if the wound became infected inside the cast, she could still face amputation. Or, at the least, nerve damage and possible paralysis.

"Well, your face is healing nicely. With a little makeup, your scars would be barely noticeable."

Katlyn perked up. "I'd hoped you'd give me some tips. Uh . . . Scott's coming by tonight." It had taken a crying jag or two and that little-girl look her mom used on Daddy sometimes to produce the desired results. But it had worked. Her parents had agreed to allow him to stop by for a visit—a very short visit.

"Then there's no time to lose!" Cissy jumped to her feet. "I've got play practice tonight, so let's get started. I'll just run back home and get my makeup kit."

Looking in the mirror for the umpteenth time, Katlyn couldn't believe it. Cissy had worked wonders with concealer, blush, a touch of mascara, and some lip gloss. But her hair still looked funny, Katlyn thought—all spiky around the shaved areas where the new growth was coming in. And the purple smudges under her eyes couldn't be completely erased—even with that stuff Cissy had ordered from a beauty magazine.

Katlyn tugged at the new top her mom had bought her at the mall and threw an afghan over her legs just as the doorbell rang. *Scott!* He was here early! He must be as excited about seeing her as she was him—or at least, she *hoped* that's what it meant.

Right after Birget had gotten Katlyn situated in the big chintz-covered chair near the window and propped her legs on the matching ottoman, she had banished the nurse from the room, threatening her within an inch of her life if she came back in while Scott was there! Now all there was left to do was—

Someone was knocking on her door. "Come in," she singsonged.

The door opened and Scott popped his head through the opening. "Are you decent?"

"As decent as I can get under the circumstances." She laughed. "Come on in."

He stepped inside and thrust out a big bouquet of flowers. "These are from"—Katlyn gasped when she saw who Scott had brought with him—"Natalie and me."

Natalie Ainsworth—looking tan and healthy! Little Miss Perfect! How could Scott do a thing like this?

"Hi, Katlyn" came the sickeningly sweet voice she loathed and detested. "How are you feeling?"

Horrible! And it's all your fault! Katlyn ground her teeth. "About the way you'd *expect* a person to feel," she snapped, "after being sentenced to bed most of the time."

She saw the look of remorse on both their faces and decided to milk it for all it was worth. After all, it was Scott's brother who had put her here!

"Actually, my life is ruined!" she wailed in as pathetic a tone as she could work up. "I'm a cripple now—an ugly cripple!" The tear oozing out from beneath one eyelid was no joke.

"No way, Katlyn," Scott said quickly. "You're still one of the prettiest girls at Shawnee High. Pretty enough to be a model . . . like Cissy."

"Not now. What kind of future is there for a person in a wheelchair?" She glanced pointedly at the monstrosity sitting in the corner where she'd made Birget wheel it. "And what guy in his right mind would look twice at me—the way I am now—except maybe to laugh?"

"*I'm* looking at you, Katlyn . . . and I'm not laughing."

Katlyn ducked her head modestly. Out of the corner of her eye, she sneaked a peek at Natalie, who seemed totally miserable. She obviously didn't like what Scott was saying. Well, good! Katlyn hadn't liked the way Natalie had stolen Scott away from her either!

"Oh, I see you got Rose's cards," Miss Ideal Christian said, moving over to a table where get-well greetings were displayed. "My little sister's only ten, you know, but I think she's pretty talented. She gets a kick out of helping Mom at the day-care center. The children worked all week on these."

"How . . . sweet," Katlyn said when Scott joined Natalie to take a look.

Katlyn shuddered as Natalie approached the bed and pulled up a chair. Why had Scott brought her along? Why couldn't it have been just the two of them?

"I know this must really be hard for you, Katlyn," Natalie was saying. *Hmph! What did* she *know about suffering?* "Sure, we all like to look our best. But God made us in His image, and it's what's on the *inside* that counts."

"Well, people don't see my *insides* when I'm lying in bed or sitting in a wheelchair."

"Some pretty important people spend a lot of time in wheelchairs."

Katlyn rolled her eyes. Would "Preacher" Ainsworth ever wind down?

But she didn't. "Have you ever heard of Joni Eareckson Tada? She broke her neck in a diving accident when she was about our age and was paralyzed from the neck down. She's been in a wheelchair ever since. But now she's a singer, a writer, and an artist—she paints fantastic pictures with a brush she holds in her teeth!"

Gross! Katlyn cringed. She'd never really cared to be around people like that. They made her nervous, and she never knew what to say. Well, now, people probably wouldn't know what to say to *her* either. One by one, her friends would find excuses for not coming around. And she'd be alone—totally alone!

Natalie broke off her monologue with a sinking feeling in the pit of her stomach. She might have known. Katlyn's accident hadn't done a thing to change her disposition. She was the same sarcastic person she'd always been. But she *had* suffered a lot, and Natalie couldn't help feeling sorry for her.

"It must be awful, Katlyn. If there's anything I can do for you . . ."

There was a slight pause. "There *is* something you can do," Katlyn said, daring her with her eyes.

Natalie was almost afraid to ask. "What is it?"

"You can cut off your hair."

"I can . . . *what*?"

"All you goody-goodys keep telling everyone how it's the 'inside that counts.' Okay, if that's true, then why don't you shave your head?"

Natalie's mouth dropped open. She knew she wasn't as pretty as her gorgeous younger sister Amy, who was a cheerleader for the Shawnee Warriors, or Scott's cousin Cissy Stiles—or even Katlyn herself. Katlyn was a beauty—even scratched up like she was and with both legs in casts. But if Natalie were to cut off all her hair, then Scott would see how really plain she was!

"Oh, she's just kidding, Nat," Scott spoke up.

Katlyn glared. "I am not! Let her *prove* to me that the outside doesn't matter."

"Well, of course it matters. But not as much as the

inside. God looks on the heart. He doesn't care if we have hair or not."

"That's easy for you to say, Natalie! You don't look like a plucked chicken!"

"Well, *that* was a bummer," Natalie told Scott when they left Katlyn's house.

He had been strangely quiet all the way home. He wouldn't even glance over at her—just kept his eyes on the road. "Yeah, maybe. But I know how she feels . . . at least a little. When Mom was drinking, I felt pretty lousy—bitter and . . . you know . . . mad—even at God. It took me a long time to turn it all over to Him. And even after I did, I was still torn up about our family. It's probably even worse for Katlyn. She really needs our help right now, Nat."

So she was right. Scott really *did* have feelings for Katlyn. He'd sure come to her defense in a hurry. But he was right about one thing: Katlyn needed a friend. "Maybe *you* can help her, Scott. But it's pretty clear she doesn't like *me*."

Scott swiveled his head to stare at her. "*Everyone* likes you, Natalie."

She couldn't look at him, had to turn her head so he wouldn't see how she felt about him. The landscape rolled by through the car window, but Natalie didn't see much of it. Scott was pretty blind, too. He didn't seem to know what Katlyn was up to. Boys could be so dense sometimes.

Still, Natalie appreciated his compliment, although the old saying, "Always a bridesmaid, never a bride," flashed through her mind. Maybe something else was also true: Always a friend, but never a *girlfriend*.

When Scott pulled to a stop in front of her house, he propped his arm on the back of her seat and lifted a lock of hair. "Don't do anything stupid, Nat."

"Oh, Scott." She sighed and reached for the door handle.

"Natalie! You won't, will you?"

"If I really thought it would help, I'd do it." She got out of there as fast as she could and rushed inside before he could see her tears of frustration.

⟨~⟩

"Natalie Ainsworth, don't you dare touch a hair of your head!" Ruthie squealed when Natalie dropped by her friend's house to spring the news after supper. "You know good and well Katlyn just wants you to look awful so Scott won't like you."

Natalie couldn't help but laugh. Ruthie's face was flushed, her rust-colored curls bobbing around her face as she shook her head in exasperation. "That girl is out to ruin you! Can't you see that?"

Natalie plopped down in a chair. "Why do Christians have such a hard time doing the right thing sometimes?" she moaned. "I just want to help Katlyn. But I'm not sure she'd be satisfied if I *did* whack off my hair." She twisted a strand around one finger, looked at it, and wrinkled her nose. "It's pretty ordinary on a *good* hair day."

"Hey, look at *this*!" Ruthie, eyes wide and flashing, uncoiled her curls and held them out on either side of her face before turning them loose to spring back into tight ringlets. "Do you know what it's like *never* to have a good hair day?" She jumped up and paced back and forth. "But the good Lord gave it to me—with a little help from my dad, who has the wildest hair in the world! Anyway, it's mine, and unless something happens to me to take it away, I intend to hang on to it!"

Natalie sighed. "Katlyn's really depressed, Ruthie. It's going to be rough when she has to start school in a wheelchair."

"I'm sorry for her. I really am. But that has nothing to do with *your hair*. If I thought it would do any good, I guess—*maybe*—I'd cut mine, too. But I know better. We've gone to school with that spoiled brat for twelve years, remember? She wouldn't even give us the time of day. Now, she wants your hair? Ha! What she wants is your *boyfriend*!"

"That's beside the point." Natalie stood to leave.

"No it's not! Suppose she wanted you to cut your *leg* off?" Ruthie finished on a note of triumph.

"We-ll." Natalie ran her fingers through her hair, realized what she was doing, and quickly dropped her hand to her side.

"Mom!" Ruthie called toward the den. "Mo-om!"

In a minute, her mother appeared in the doorway. "What in the world do you want, Ruthie? Can't you come find me and speak in a civilized tone?"

"Sorry. But I've got to go to Natalie's, Mom. She's got a big problem, and I can't leave her till it's solved."

Natalie glanced helplessly at Mrs. Ryan and spread her hands.

"Can *I* do anything to help, Natalie?"

Ruthie spoke for her. "We're trying to decide whether to cut off her hair or break her leg."

"Ruthie!" Natalie groaned.

"Come on, Nat. Let's go!" Ruthie grabbed Natalie's arm.

Mrs. Ryan looked confused. "How long will you be gone, honey?"

Ruthie shrugged. "Maybe for the rest of the summer—or maybe for our entire senior year. But we'll take it one day at a time. Is it okay if I spend the night, Natalie . . . Mom?"

"Now, Ruthie, you know my cosmetology class is in the morning and your dad goes to work. So I'd have to drop Justin off with you at the Ainsworths, and I'm not sure . . ."

"Don't worry about it, Mrs. Ryan," Natalie put in. "Dad loves to make breakfast for a mob. He's always wired up when he comes home from work, anyway, so he won't be going to bed right away."

Ruthie grabbed Natalie's hand and headed for the door. "Guess it's all set then, okay, Mom? Just make sure Monster leaves his snakes here! See ya!"

"Sssss. Sssss. Sssss."

Natalie's eyes popped open at the strange sound next to her pillow. She found herself staring into two slitted eyes. "Yikes!" she screamed, almost breaking her neck getting to the other side of the bed, where Ruthie had been sleeping.

Ruthie yelped, dumped Natalie onto the floor, and fell on top of her, one of her legs becoming tangled in the sheet on the way down.

Justin was laughing hysterically as he climbed onto

the bed and hissed, wiggling the long, black snake with its red, forked tongue in their faces.

"Get that thing away from me!" Natalie yelled.

"I'm gonna kill you," Ruthie threatened. "If Natalie doesn't kill *me* first." She climbed off Natalie, who proceeded to untangle herself from the bedsheets. "What are you doing up here anyway? This is not your home—and it's Natalie's bedroom!"

"Mr. A. said for someone to say 'come down to breakfast.'" The seven-year-old grinned, displaying appled cheeks covered with freckles, and wiggled the snake toward them again. "*I'm* someone!"

"You're gonna be *mud* if you don't get off that bed," Ruthie warned. She lunged for him, but he scooted away, ran out of the room and down the stairs.

They heard a scream from the direction of the living room where Jill Ainsworth would be doing her morning aerobics with the TV. "Justin's found Mom." Natalie laughed.

By the time the two reached the kitchen, Justin was on the floor, moaning and groaning in between giggles as Natalie's dad tickled him unmercifully.

"Oh, this is so embarrassing!" Ruthie wailed. "Why couldn't my parents have been satisfied with one child? Monster, get up from there!"

"Males are different from females," Jill announced, coming in from the living room with Amy, Sarah, and Rose right behind. "They enjoy the strangest things."

"Like driving females crazy, for one thing," Ruthie said.

"Oh, come on now," Jim said, eyeing Jill's trim figure, "if you got yourself a snake and did those contortions, you wouldn't have to exercise with the TV every morning."

"No, because I'd be permanently out of shape," she retorted.

"Some of the stuff we do at cheerleading practice is not too much different from that," Amy said, helping set the table.

"I don't see what's so funny." That was Sarah, the twelve-year-old, Natalie's "serious" sister.

"I bet Pongo would like to play with it," Rose claimed.

Justin unraveled himself and stuck the snake behind his back. "That mutt's not getting my snake!"

"Okay, what's everyone having?" Jim asked, banging on the griddle with his spatula. Natalie had never been able to figure out how her dad could work all night as a correctional officer at the federal prison and still be in a good mood when he got home.

When the orders were served, Natalie slid into a chair beside Ruthie and waited for everyone to pipe down for the blessing.

Afterward, when her dad asked if anyone had a verse for the day, Justin spoke up. "I do. It goes like this: Sister Ruthie jumped in the lake, swallowed a snake, and came back out with a bellyache. Har, har!" He laughed, pointing his finger in Ruthie's face.

"Not *that* kind of verse, Monster!" she retorted, rolling her eyes. "You know Mr. A. means a *Bible* verse."

"Ah, cut him some slack, Ruthie. He's just being a boy," Natalie's dad replied.

Her mom poured him some more coffee. "Now I know why I had all girls."

"*I* have a verse, Mr. A.," Ruthie spoke up after the giggles died down. "I don't remember every word, but it's something like: 'It's a sin for a woman to cut her hair.'"

"Is this some kind of joke, Ruthie?" Jill asked as Natalie shot her friend a warning look and her sisters looked up with puzzled frowns on their faces.

The sparks flew in Ruthie's brown eyes as she related what Katlyn had challenged Natalie to do.

"Oh, she couldn't have meant it."

"She did, though. I think Katlyn wants Natalie to look ugly so Scott won't like her."

"If that's her reason, Nat," Amy began, "I wouldn't give her the satisfaction!"

Natalie took a deep breath. "Maybe that's not the reason. She just feels so ugly. You know how pretty Katlyn was before the accident. Well, she still is, but it's going to take something really dramatic to convince *her*."

"I'd cut *my* hair if it would make her feel better," sweet little Rose said. "All the kids at the day-care center have been making cards for her. We hoped that would help."

"I know they did. I saw them. They're really good, Rosie," Natalie complimented her.

"My mom could cut your hair for you," Justin offered. "She's a . . . a cos-me-not, or something like that."

Ruthie groaned. "Cosmetologist, you mean."

"I read in the paper about this boy who had cancer and his hair fell out," Sarah spoke up for the first time. "All the kids in his class shaved their heads so he wouldn't feel bad when he started back to school."

"What a nice thing to do," Jill said.

"Yeah, but when the boy with no hair walked in, *he* was wearing a wig."

Rose giggled, and another round of laughter broke out.

"This is different," Ruthie insisted. "Katlyn is jealous of Natalie. She shouldn't get away with it!"

Natalie pondered for a minute. "Okay, if I did cut my hair and Scott was turned off, wouldn't that prove Katlyn's point—that the outside *does* make a difference?"

"If your hair fell out because of cancer treatments or some accident, that would be one thing," her mother argued, "but Ruthie's right. There's no point in going to extremes just to prove something to an ill-tempered girl."

"Right," her dad agreed. "Wouldn't that mean we should all shave our heads, or that all you ugly women should go without makeup?"

Before he was mobbed, he put up his hands to defend himself. "Just kidding. But seriously, what Katlyn is asking is ridiculous. It's like saying you should stop eating because physical food isn't as important as spiritual food."

"*I* say: Hide the scissors, the knives, the saws, the—"

"Oh, Ruthie!" Natalie gave her friend a quick hug. "Maybe I could pull out the hairs one by—"

The ringing of the doorbell ended what she was about to say.

Justin jumped up. "I'll get it."

In a second he returned, followed by Scott, wearing jeans, his White Dove T-shirt, and a baseball cap. Po-

lite as always, Scott reached for his cap. When he removed it, there was a chorus of gasps.

His beautiful, dark, wavy hair was gone!

His head was as bare as a newborn baby's bottom.

Seven

Natalie couldn't believe her eyes. "Scott!"

"I got to thinking about it. Maybe Katlyn was serious, but she had no right to ask you to cut off your hair. After all, it was a member of *my* family who hurt her."

Natalie sank back into her chair. Justin, eyes wide as flying saucers, gaped up at him. Everyone else sat, dumbstruck, gazes glued to Scott's bald head. Scott Lambert—chief hunk and just about the most gorgeous guy at Shawnee High!

"Wanna see my snake?" Justin asked, breaking the silence. "He don't bite."

Scott managed a little smile. "Good thing. I couldn't take that so soon after being scalped." He rubbed his head self-consciously and put the cap back on. "I'm stopping by to see Katlyn, Nat, so I'll be late getting to the Johnsons' house to work on the project. Would you tell Andy for me?"

"Sure," Natalie squeaked, barely able to answer.

"Wow!" Ruthie said after Scott left and the breath returned to her lungs. "He must really be crazy about you, Nat, to go *that* far."

Natalie wasn't so sure. *Is he crazy about* me—*or Katlyn Chander?*

⁓

Katlyn had been expecting Scott, so she wasn't surprised to hear his deep voice rumbling in the downstairs hall when Mrs. Jennings let him in. She just hoped he wasn't bringing Miss Prim and Proper with him! But she was totally unprepared for what she saw when Scott stepped through her door.

"Wh-what happened to you?"

Could this really be Scott? He looked thinner—more like Zac. But there was no smile, no caring look. Only a motionless, expressionless mask.

"Hi, Katlyn." He came on into the room.

She could only stare as he pulled a chair over to her bed and sat down. "What . . . did you . . . do?" she whispered. All that beautiful thick hair was gone. There was only a shiny scalp that made his nose and ears look bigger. "Why?"

"Don't you understand? This has nothing to do with Natalie. It's *my* family who hurt you. You see, Katlyn, Nat's right. It's the inside that counts. Unless . . . being bald makes me look ugly to you or something."

"Are you trying to make me feel guilty?"

"Of course not. This is no fun for me, Katlyn. No more than being laid up for the rest of the summer is for you. Believe me, I don't even want to lose my hair when I get *old*! I just wanted you to know that none of us feels any differently about you now than we did before the accident . . . except that I'm sorry it happened.

And especially that my *brother* did it."

Katlyn believed him. Scott Lambert was about the most honest guy she knew. She felt terrible. She'd wanted to strike out at Natalie—make *her* look bad. But she hadn't meant for *Scott* to take her up on her dare.

"Thanks," she whimpered. "But . . . I hope you'll let it grow out."

"If that's what you want."

He looked into her eyes—like he could see all the way into the darkest corner of her heart. Could he really tell how she felt about Natalie? About him? She scrunched down in her chair, feeling about two inches tall—as low as a snake crawling along on its belly. She didn't hear much more and barely noticed when he excused himself to go to work on the youth project.

Katlyn was only too glad to see Lorna Nolan when she dropped by later in the day on her way to a meeting in town. "I don't know what to make of all this," she confessed, propping herself up in bed. After Scott left, she'd been too drained to sit in the chair anymore.

"Try. How do you feel, Katlyn?"

She took a deep breath, looked up toward the ceiling, and blinked. "Rotten."

"Would you be willing to cut off your hair for Natalie if the situation were reversed?"

Katlyn swallowed hard and shook her head. "No . . . I wouldn't. And I'm real sorry *Scott* did."

"He did it to show his concern for you, not to make you feel guilty."

"He probably did it for *Natalie*, which makes me

feel *jealous*!" she snapped. "Before the accident, I was prettier than she is. I *know* I was. I wanted him to see her without hair . . . so he wouldn't want to go out with her." *Now I sound like the Wicked Witch of the West!* Katlyn thought.

Dr. Nolan crossed her long, slender legs, waited quietly for a moment, and asked softly, "Then what is it about Natalie that Scott likes, if not her looks?"

Katlyn felt her lip trembling and bit down on it. "Well, she's not exactly ugly. But Scott . . ." She fell back onto her pillow and closed her eyes. "I know what you want me to say. The same thing Natalie wants me to say. And those youth directors. And Scott. Okay! There's something *inside* that girl that appeals to him. Maybe it's her personality. . . ."

"That's what he likes about her?"

Katlyn drew a deep breath and opened her eyes. "He's had a lot of problems in his family, so he turned to God. I think he sees Natalie as some kind of saint or something."

"You really believe that, Katlyn?"

"Not exactly," she admitted. "But he does like the idea that she's a Christian who doesn't mind talking about her . . . faith. I think he needs that to hang on to."

"Well, let's see," the psychologist said thoughtfully. "It wouldn't work if you said you were a Christian just to attract Scott, would it?"

Katlyn growled and turned her eyes toward the wall. "Don't expect *me* to go around spouting all that religious stuff!"

"What's wrong with that?"

Katlyn turned her head to stare at Lorna Nolan. "*You* don't shout to everyone, 'Hey, look at me! I'm a psychologist. I got my life together, so why don't you get yours together,' do you?"

Dr. Nolan laughed. "No, but I do let it be known that I'm a counselor, and when my name is spoken or written, it's usually preceded by my title, 'doctor.' "

Katlyn shrugged. "That's your *job*."

"What about a minister?"

"Well, sure. But Natalie is just a sixteen-year-old high school student, for Pete's sake."

"Yes, but maybe her desire to be a Christian is as strong as your desire to be a model. Perhaps Christian ministry is her career goal."

Katlyn glared at her. "Whose side are you on anyway?"

"It's not a matter of sides, Katlyn. But I'm on your side. That's why I'm here. To help you reason things out and put them in proper perspective." Dr. Nolan uncrossed her legs and rose. "Now I've got to run. Think about it, and we'll talk some more next week when I'm in town."

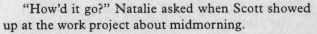

"How'd it go?" Natalie asked when Scott showed up at the work project about midmorning.

"Okay, I guess. Katlyn wants me to let my hair grow out."

Natalie handed him a hammer and stole a glance at him. He looked so pathetic, she couldn't resist breaking into a laugh.

"Looks pretty dumb, huh?"

"Not really. I think what you did was a wonderful gesture." Actually, it was more than that. It was quite a sacrifice. Not many guys would have done something like that for anyone. *Unless it happened to be someone . . . very special.*

They worked on in silence for a while before Scott spoke up again. "How do you feel about bald-headed guys? Would you go out with one?"

Was Scott asking her for a date? No way. He'd just come from seeing Katlyn. "Depends," she answered evasively.

He seemed surprised and almost missed a nail. "On what? Aren't people the same no matter how they look?"

"Maybe . . . maybe not. A sixteen-year-old who's bald may have some kind of disease and might not feel like doing much of anything but lying around. And someone who shaved his head could have some pretty weird ideas—like maybe he's a member of some cult or something."

"Let's get real, Natalie. Maybe you think *I'm* ugly now that I'm bald!"

She lifted her eyebrows. "Weren't you ugly before?"

"Whoa! I guess I asked for that one, didn't I?"

She didn't answer, just kept on hammering. Scott Lambert had to know what all the girls thought about him!

"Oh, well, I'll just keep wearing this cap until my hair grows out. Besides, most people haven't even noticed."

She cocked her head, grinning over at him. "If

80

you're coming Wednesday night to the youth meeting, they will. Andy and Stephanie don't allow caps inside the church."

He reached over and yanked her ponytail, dodging her hand as she grabbed for his cap. "Time out for a water break! Race you to the maple tree!"

———

"I don't believe it—yes, I do," Ruthie contradicted herself as Natalie parked the car in the church lot on Wednesday evening. "Speaking of hairdos—and don'ts—get a load of *that*."

Natalie slid out from behind the wheel and stood to see what had blown Ruthie's mind this time. Stick, the tall, lanky star of the Shawnee Warriors, was strutting his stuff on the outdoor basketball court. The younger boys trotted alongside their idol, doing their best to steal the ball. The funny part, Natalie thought, was that every one of them had had his hair cut just like Stick's—in a flattop about three inches long and sticking straight up all over his head!

"After all this talk about the inside counting most," she said, "I guess we can be glad Stick's basically a nice guy and a good influence."

"Yeah. Too bad we can't say the same thing about Zac Lambert."

Natalie was silent as they entered the ground floor of the church and found the room where the youth group would be holding their first meeting since Katlyn's accident. In fact, she thought, trying to keep her mind on her business as president of the group, that was what had triggered their decision to study alcohol abuse for several weeks. So tonight should be pretty interesting. She wondered what Officer Burns would have to say. He'd been great at the jail in Oakwood the night of the accident—hadn't made her feel like a criminal at all. She was really grateful that he'd agreed to come speak to them on such short notice.

Sure enough, when she and Ruthie got inside, all the buzz was about Katlyn Chander and what had happened over the Fourth-of-July weekend. Ruthie looked around for her boyfriend, Sean, who usually worked late for a local food chain and couldn't make the meetings. But Cissy and Scott were there. Though not members of this church, their Aunt Martha Brysen—the rock of the family—was. And Natalie knew they were all closer since the awful storm that had ripped through Garden City and changed so many lives—including Cissy's and Scott's.

When Andy rapped on a table, the talk died down and everyone shifted his or her attention to the front of the room. "It's no secret what's on everyone's mind tonight. Katlyn Chander's accident was a terrible tragedy. Even though she's not a member of our youth group, most of you know her. And *all* of you know the Lambert family since Scott gave his testimony here at our church a couple of months ago."

Every head turned toward Scott and Cissy, sitting near the door. Natalie knew how embarrassed he was with all eyes focused on him. A red flush stained his cheeks and didn't stop at the dark shadow of his hairline, but crept up until it covered his whole scalp! Poor Scott! She wouldn't blame him if he took off and never came back.

"Tonight," Andy went on, "we have a guest speaker for our first session in a new series of our White Dove campaign. But before I introduce him, let me just say what we've been saying all along: Living a pure life is not a matter of sexual purity only. In other words, it's not just what we *do* with our bodies, it's what we put *into* them. Officer Jim Burns of the Oakwood P. D. is here to tell us what happens when people—especially teenagers—drink and drive."

Natalie gave Officer Burns a welcoming smile as he stood to speak, twirling his police cap in his hand before he laid it on the table in front of him. "You already know what I do and why I'm here. So I'll get right to it. My job as a law-enforcement officer is not getting paid for playing cops-and-robbers. It's down and dirty and gives me a look at life I'd just as soon never see. But I'm a Christian, too, and as the old saying goes, 'Someone's got to do it.' So why not someone who really cares about people? As you know, policemen are having an image problem these days, and for some of us, it's a bum rap." There were a few snickers, and Officer Burns paused before going on.

"When the Chander accident occurred, I was the booking officer on duty when Mr. Lambert and Miss Ainsworth here came in. It was the young lady—Natalie—who invited me here to give you a few tips on how to prevent what happened that night.

"You've all read the reports in the paper, but what the journalists never capture completely is what it's like to see an accident up close and personal. I hope you never do. And one way you can guarantee that is *never* to drink and drive.

"I'm not going to get into all the theology about drinking. That's Andy's and Stephanie's job"—he glanced over at the good-looking couple sitting together over to the side—"but I do want to say that nobody starts out wanting to become addicted to anything—alcohol, drugs, prescription or otherwise. When certain substances get into our systems, they can take control."

Reaching over, Officer Burns picked up two handsful of brochures and gestured for a couple of the guys to pass them out. "I got permission from AA—Alcoholics Anonymous—to distribute these at your meeting. This is a twelve-question quiz to help you determine if you, or someone you know, has a drinking problem. If you can answer 'yes' to any of these questions, you need to take a serious look at what you're doing."

When the brochures were handed out, Natalie scanned the first few questions:

1. Do you drink because you have problems? To relax?
2. Do you drink when you get mad at other people, your friends, or parents?
3. Do you prefer to drink alone?
4. Are your grades starting to slip? Are you goofing off on your job?
5. Do you think it's "cool" to be able to hold your liquor?

"Take the brochure home with you and study it," the officer continued, waiting while papers rustled and the group flipped through the pages. "If any of these apply to you, please get help. Call a friend from church, or discuss it with your pastor or one of your youth leaders." There was another long pause. "I'd hate to see *you* down where I work, waiting to be booked for DUI on possible felony charges. But worse than that is the sentence a drunk driver hands himself when he harms an innocent bystander or passenger: Having to live with the fact—every day of his life—that the person he's injured may never walk again . . . or may not live."

Zac was late for his appointment at the Rehab Center. But since he hadn't told his family what he'd been up to, he'd had to wait until they all scattered for the night—Scott, to the youth group at Natalie's church, where he'd been attending all summer; Mom, to her AA meeting. It had worked great for Zac to ride in to the hospital with his dad, who was making late evening rounds. Now, if Terri and Chad just hadn't given up on him. . . .

"Hey, you guys!" he called as he burst through the doors into the big room, deserted now except for the little eight-year-old sitting in his wheelchair and the receptionist who filled in as a therapist some nights. "Sorry I'm late!"

Terri set his mind at ease. "No problem. We just got here ourselves. Chad's aunt had to work the night shift, so this was the only time he could come today."

"Hi, Zac!" This kid had a fantastic smile. Made you feel better just to hang around him. "You'll never guess what I can do! I've been practicing all week. But we waited till you got here to get started."

Zac ruffled the fuzz on top of the boy's head. Without his cap, Chad's nearly bald pate looked something like a furry cue ball. "Okay, champ, show me."

With Terri's help, the little boy struggled out of his wheelchair and hopped over to the parallel bars. She positioned the prosthesis to replace his missing limb, buckled it on, then led him to the bars. Holding on to the chrome rail, he took a step on his good leg, then brought the artificial limb alongside and put the foot down. When he had balanced his full weight, he took another step. Slowly he made it to the end of the mat, then turned with a triumphant grin. "I did it! I did it, Zac! I'm walking!"

Zac could hardly see for the dumb tears in his eyes.

Eight

"I'm sick and tired of being cooped up in this house!" Katlyn griped to Cissy when she dropped by the next day. "Can't walk, can't drive, can't swim, can't date—as if any guy would ask me if I *could* get out of here!"

Cissy, looking like a cover of *Mademoiselle* magazine, was sympathetic. "I know it must be awful for you. But when are you going to believe it's who you *are* instead of how you *look* that's important?"

"Ohh, don't remind me." Katlyn covered her face with her hands. "Who I *am* right now is not so hot either. Haven't you seen Scott's head?"

Cissy nodded. "I can't imagine anyone else doing such a thing. Scott's pretty terrific—even if he is my cousin."

"I didn't ask him to do that, Cissy. I was just so mad at Natalie for saying what you just said—that the outside doesn't make a difference—when I know good and well it *does*!"

"Well, sure it does, Katlyn. But I've learned a lot since that episode last spring, remember? I had gotten so caught up in myself—what *I* wanted, what was important to *me*—that I wasn't thinking of anyone else. There I was—a senior in high school, feeling so grown-up, everyone telling me how beautiful and talented I was. So when my parents wouldn't pay for me to go to New York and pursue an acting career, I got mad and decided to elope with Ron and . . . well, you know the rest."

"Yeah, what a jerk. Ran off and left you in the middle of a tornado!" Katlyn sighed and thrashed around on the bed, trying to get comfortable. "And his friend—the one I dated a couple of times—hasn't called or sent a card or anything. A lot *he* cared."

"That's what I mean, Kat. They were great-looking guys, but that's all they had going for them."

"Zac is a hunk, too—and look what *he* did to me. I feel like I've been robbed," Katlyn moaned.

Cissy brushed a wisp of blond hair out of her eyes. "I know how you feel. I was sure my parents had ruined my chances forever when they wouldn't let me go to the big city. But now I know they were right. I need to get my education first and prepare myself for whatever the future holds. Who knows?" She smiled. "I may make it yet, although I'm no great actress. I think it's the applause I really like."

"Nothing wrong with that, is there?"

"No-o. But when I was out in that storm with no one to turn to but God, I realized my ambitions were pretty lame. If I'd died, I wouldn't have been ready to meet the Lord. I'm glad it happened, though, because it forced me to take a good look at my priorities. Before, *I* was the center of my world. Now *God* is."

Katlyn frowned. "You're beginning to sound like Natalie."

"I take that as a compliment."

Cissy was positively *glowing*, Katlyn fumed to herself. What was it with this Natalie Ainsworth?

"In fact, it was Natalie who gave me *this* the night of the storm." She pulled a tiny gold chain from under her top. Dangling from the chain was a miniature dove, wings spread as if in flight.

"Oh, *that*." Katlyn shrugged. "She gave me one, too. Left it on my pillow when I was unconscious in the hospital in Oakwood. It's around here somewhere, I guess. But what good did it do me?"

Cissy pulled her chair up closer to the bed. "But don't you see, Kat? This little dove is the answer. Or at least it symbolizes the answer! It's God's Spirit who can change things—not the psychologist, not the doctors, not even the minister."

Oh, brother! Cissy, too? The girl Katlyn admired most in the whole world! But Cissy wasn't through yet.

"You know, with God, something good can come from the worst things that happen to us."

Katlyn was furious. "Name *one* good thing that's come out of my accident!"

"I can do better than that. For one thing, it's caused Aunt Helen to face up to her alcoholism and do something about it. For another, it's brought the whole family closer together . . . well, everyone but Zac."

Cissy's gaze took on a faraway look. "And there's another thing. I know you don't think so now, but things could have been worse. Suppose Zac hadn't left the party, and you'd stayed at your lake house with him? You guys were inside a long time alone as it was. . . ."

Katlyn almost came off the bed. "Just exactly *what* are you accusing me of, Cissy Stiles?"

"Nothing, Kat. I think it's great if you and Zac are . . . more than friends. But . . . things can happen . . . especially when you're drinking."

"Who said we were 'more than friends'? And how did *you*—" Katlyn broke off, feeling an incriminating blush heating her cheeks. Cissy was nice enough not to notice.

"I guess I'm really talking about myself, Kat. If Ron and I hadn't been stopped by the tornado that night, we'd have gotten married . . . *if* we'd been able to find someone to perform the ceremony. If not . . . I'm afraid we'd have ended up in a motel somewhere. Now, what would *that* have done for my future?"

Katlyn couldn't look Cissy in the eye. The older girl had always been really nice to her. But she hadn't expected Cissy to be so blunt.

"Tell you what," Cissy said brightly. "If you're up to it by then, why don't you come to the play Friday night? You can be my guest of honor and sit right up front."

It was tempting. Any other time . . . "Thanks, Cissy, but no thanks. I've been out a few times, and everyone stares at me. I'd rather wait until my scars have faded more. Besides, Daddy doesn't want me out in crowds. He's afraid someone might bump my legs or something. But I'd like to hear all about it."

That was all the prompting Cissy needed to spring into action. She began to recite some of her lines, striking poses, using her fake accent until Katlyn had to laugh in spite of herself.

And when Birget popped her head in the door, she was shocked. "So, it *vass* laughter I heard out in the hallvay? I thought you vere cryink!"

Cissy was entranced. "Are you Swedish, by any chance? I could use some help with my 'Swedish maid' accent."

And then they were off. Katlyn couldn't get a word in edgewise. Before long, the two of them were jabbering like they'd known each other forever. Birget even told them about her life in Sweden—how her parents had died when she was fifteen, and she'd come to America to live with an aunt and uncle.

"Thanks be to the good Lord that I haff a good job. Maybe someday I can haff my own little apartment, too."

"What a treasure, Kat!" Cissy said when Miss Birget finally left the room. "You know, I'd love for her to come to the play, too. But if you guys don't make it, she could wheel you over Friday night afterward. I forgot to tell you my parents are giving a party for the cast at our house."

"Who'll be there?"

"Oh, the usual crowd—the ones who are in town, that is. And the players, of course." Cissy grimaced. "And then there's Aunt Martha, Aunt Helen and Uncle Lawrence, Scott . . . and probably Zac," she finished in a whisper.

"Then count me out!" Katlyn was adamant. "My dad would never stand for me to be in the same house with that guy!"

I should have bitten my tongue off before I mentioned

91

the Lamberts to Katlyn! Cissy thought on the way home. But she'd asked, so what else was there to do? It was obvious, though, that Katlyn was nowhere near ready to forgive Zac for what he'd done to her.

In the kitchen, Cissy got out a glass, filled it with ice, then went to the refrigerator to pour herself some lemonade. She'd sit in the shade on the patio and go over the script one more time.

But before she could exit through the French doors leading to the pool, the housekeeper stopped her. "Miss Cissy, you have a letter on the tray in the foyer."

"Thanks, Cornelia." Cissy set her glass down and went to check the mail.

She flipped through the letters. Most were for her mom and dad. A couple addressed to Occupant. And one . . . "What's this?"

Her heart was pounding as she picked up the letter opener. With shaky fingers, she sliced open the flap and took out the letter. It was brief and to the point. More information would follow after they received her reply.

"I am *not* believing this!"

Why *now*—when Katlyn was in such bad shape? If Cissy answered the letter, it would seem so crass—so selfish.

She'd like to run it by her parents. But she wasn't sure how they'd react. And her friends would only say, "Go for it!" Maybe Scott? He had a good head on his shoulders—even if he didn't have any hair on it at the moment, she thought with a wry smile.

Funny, it was Natalie Ainsworth she most wanted to talk to. She might be a little younger than Cissy's crowd, but that girl was wise beyond her years. She'd know what to do.

As she sat out by the pool going over her lines, Cissy's mind kept wandering. "Stop it!" she reprimanded herself out loud. "You're letting a silly letter take over your life!"

Then it dawned on her. The perfect time to mention the letter would be at the cast party after the play. Everyone would be there, so she could get their input then.

It was settled then. She'd do it. Friday night.

When Scott and Natalie arrived at the Stiles mansion in Garden Acres after the play, Natalie couldn't help glancing over at the Chander house next door. The upstairs was dark. Katlyn hadn't made it to the performance. Maybe she was already in bed. Poor thing! She was missing out on so much fun this summer.

But when Cissy's other friends began to arrive, Natalie forgot all about Katlyn. Why was it that this crowd always made her feel like a space alien? It wasn't just what they were wearing, which was the latest, most "in" fashions, of course. It was the way they moved— like they were gliding instead of walking—and the way they tossed their hair. Little things like that.

Cissy came late. Natalie supposed she'd had to change and remove her stage makeup. But even with the applause that broke out when she was spotted, Cissy passed by everyone else with a smile and a wave before plopping down right beside *Natalie*! "How'd you like the play, Nat?"

"It was great, Cissy. You're really talented."

"Well, thanks, but don't go 'way. We've got to talk," the older girl whispered behind her hand, then gave a sigh. "But I guess I'd better circulate."

With Scott off somewhere, Natalie took a moment to look around the crowded pool area. Tiny lights twinkled in all the trees, and banks of flowers bloomed almost to the water's edge. The place looked like a fairyland.

"Having a good time?" She looked up to find Amanda Brooke, one of the models from Belk's, where Cissy occasionally did some modeling. "Cissy has been telling me about something that's going on at your church this summer—White Dove, I think she called it. She's pretty excited about it."

Before Natalie could answer, Scott was back with refreshments and a portfolio under one arm. It turned out to be blowups of some pictures he'd taken of the work project—before-and-after shots of the Johnson place and a few others. He'd caught some of the youth off guard in some neat candids, too.

"Wow, Scott!" Amanda looked over his shoulder as he brought out the pictures one by one. "These are good—*really* good. Cissy didn't tell me she had a photographer in the family."

"Hmm." He flashed the dazzling grin that always made Natalie's knees grow weak. He might not have much hair, but he still looked great to her. "Wonder why she failed to mention *that*. Some of my best stuff was of Cissy."

"Oh, you!" Amanda threw back her head and laughed. "How does it feel, Nat, to be seen in public with an egotist who looks like a skinhead?"

Natalie began to relax. These people weren't so bad—they just had different priorities. And Amanda, at least, had seemed really interested in the White Dove program.

There was a lot of conversation and laughter and plenty of compliments on Cissy's rendition of the hilarious maid. One of them was from Cissy's Aunt Martha. "Well, my dear, you outdid yourself tonight. You deserve an Academy Award for that performance."

Natalie could see that Cissy could hardly believe her ears. Aunt Martha wasn't known for flattery. She always told the absolute truth, even if it *was* sometimes a little hard to take.

All eyes turned toward the older woman, standing tall and straight, her softly waved white hair catching the light. "Only a great actress could have pulled off the part of a maid so well. I happen to know you haven't done a lick of work in your life!"

After a moment of stunned silence, there were hoots of laughter and good-natured ribbing. Then Cissy disappeared for a minute, returning with a letter she was waving in her hand.

"Well, *someone* else likes me," she retorted, finding a spot where she could be seen and heard. "I hadn't planned to do this—make it public, I mean. But since most of my friends and family are here, I really need to hear what all of you have to say when I get through reading this letter."

Everyone edged nearer. Natalie could have heard a pin drop as Cissy began:

Dear Miss Stiles,

This is to inform you that, based on the photo sent to us in January and your contest entry blank, you have been selected as one of the top ten finalists in our Dream Teen Model Search.

This means you are invited to come to New York, all expenses paid, in late November to compete for selection of the top three models.

With this announcement comes a certificate entitling you to a $500 shopping spree at Macy's. As a special promotion, Macy's will also be sponsoring a float featuring our ten finalists in their annual Thanksgiving Day parade.

Please respond within two weeks so that if you are unable to participate, we can select another contestant. Upon your acceptance of this offer, we will send further details.

> *Congratulations and best wishes,*
> *Marlena Minotti, Coordinator*

There was not a sound except for the hum of the pool filter and the chirping of a few night birds.

Cissy refolded the letter and looked up, her clear blue eyes wide. "What do *you* think I should do?"

"Watch this! Watch this!"

Zac broke the surface of the Rehab Center pool just in time to see Chad bend over the side—headfirst—and push off with his good leg. He came up, sputtering and laughing, dog-paddling like mad to escape the wave Zac splashed in his direction.

"Terrific dive, pal! But we need to work on that

stroke if you're going to make it to the Olympics by the time you're old enough."

Zac hadn't been able to get the little guy off his mind. What a trooper. With Chad's aunt working the night shift lately and his brother—the one who was supposed to be watching the boy—off no telling where, the rehab staff had been allowing him to use the pool at odd hours—as long as there was a certified lifeguard on duty. Having been a lifeguard at the country club a few summers in high school, Zac had jumped at the chance. It hadn't hurt to drop a few names to the hospital staff, though. By now everyone knew he was Dr. Lambert's son anyway.

"Zac, you're not paying 'tention. Watch this back flip." With that, Chad proceeded to execute a slightly awkward backward roll in the water.

"Awesome!" Zac applauded. "Come on, I'll race you to the other end!"

The Olympic-sized pool and surrounding paved area connected to the therapy rooms through a covered walkway, wide enough for wheelchairs and other equipment to be rolled through easily. Overhead, a glass canopy admitted the sunlight during all seasons, while keeping the temperature of the water a few degrees warmer than usual. Here, arthritis patients did their water aerobics, and others—at different stages of recovery from other diseases—swam laps to strengthen unused muscles, or sat in front of huge jets that propelled the water at great force.

"Swimming is the best exercise we know for most people, but that's not anything new to you," Terri had told Zac. "We want Chad to feel as much like a normal boy as possible. He's having fun while using the muscles he has left in his bad leg and keeping the others toned."

Well, Zac doubted if there was any swimming pool in the Projects. And until the trial, at least, he planned to see that this little guy had all the fun he could stand!

Nine

At Cissy's announcement, murmurs rippled through the group like waves rolling onto a beach.

She gave them a minute, then struck a pose. "Vell, vhat would a Svedish maid do with $500 in the Big Apple anyvay?"

A few chuckles eased the tension. "Good try, darling," Elizabeth Stiles said, "but I don't believe a word of it. This would be the *first* time you ever failed to get excited about a shopping spree. You're too much like your mother, I'm afraid." She cocked an eyebrow at her husband, waiting for a retort.

He didn't disappoint her. "Spending money like water runs in this family." John Stiles gave his daughter a curious look. "So you don't want to take them up on it, baby?"

"Well, sure, I'd love to. I think it would be great fun. But modeling is no longer the only goal in life for me. You're right, Dad, Mom—about what you said earlier. I need to finish my education first. Then, if God wants me to go into acting or modeling as a career, okay. But I'm not pushing for it anymore."

Cissy didn't miss the cool looks exchanged by some

of her society friends. Everyone, that is, except Amanda Brooke, who seemed eager to hear more.

"But you entered the contest," her mother went on.

"Well, you see, they didn't want professional pictures. They wanted snapshots. Scott took some that turned out pretty good—"

"*Pretty* good?" Scott prodded.

Cissy laughed. "Okay, Scott, they were *great*. It was really your photography that caught the judge's eye. Had nothing to do with *me*," she cracked, then grew serious again. "But I entered the contest back in January, before my . . . um . . . rendezvous with Ron and the tornado."

John Stiles paced the area around the pool. "Well, honey, that was quite a different matter. Your mother and I didn't want you traipsing off to New York, hoping for a break that might never come."

Her mom was watching her dad closely as she said, "I think it's a wonderful opportunity for you, Cissy. Besides, if you don't go, you'd always wonder where it might have led."

Cissy's heart began to thud. "You mean . . . you two wouldn't mind?"

"As long as you don't let your head get too far into the clouds, and keep your feet on the ground," her father deadpanned.

"Oh, don't worry, Dad. Summer theater and modeling a little have taught me that there's a lot of work that goes into either career. . . ." She scanned the faces, searching for one in particular. "There's someone else I'd like to hear from, though. What do *you* think, Natalie?"

Natalie jumped, probably not expecting to be singled out of the crowd. "Me? Well, you know what I think of you, Cissy—your looks, your talent. But there's something else, too." She seemed to hesitate. "Maybe God *wants* you to go to New York City. Maybe He was just waiting for you to turn everything over to Him before He opened a door. You could always pray that He'd close it if He didn't want you to walk through."

Cissy nodded. Leave it to Natalie to cut right through the confusion. She knew she could count on her. Still . . . "There *is* one other thing that worries me." The crowd seemed to be holding its breath. "Katlyn."

"What's Katlyn got to do with it?" someone spoke up.

"Well, after preaching about the inside being more important than the outside, how can I tell her I'm a finalist in a *modeling* competition?"

"I know what you mean," Natalie said. "When she dared me to cut off all my hair, I really considered doing it—at least for a little while."

"Well, no one has to wonder what *I* did to prove that point!" Scott said, rubbing his hand over the stubble that was beginning to grow back.

Cissy's face fell. "So that leaves me right back where I started."

"No, it doesn't, honey." Her mom stepped forward and put her arm around Cissy's shoulders. "I hope this doesn't sound harsh, but I don't think you should cripple your own life just because Katlyn is crippled. I agree that we need to help her all we can, but we can't live her life for her. You're also obligated to take advantage of your *own* opportunities when they come along."

"I agree with your mom, Cissy," Natalie spoke up. "I don't think it would help Katlyn for you to turn down this offer—just like I didn't think cutting off my hair would make any real difference in the long run."

"*Now* you tell me," Scott muttered under his breath, bringing some chuckles.

"So, Cissy, the ball is in your court," her dad said, coming to join them beside the pool, the lantern light reflecting in the smooth surface of the water. "But whatever you decide, your mother and I will support you all the way."

"Well, just pray that Katlyn will understand. . . ." Cissy murmured, looking over at the darkened room on the second floor of the Chander house.

Was Katlyn there now, looking back at her, watching all the beautiful people walking about on their two good legs?

Katlyn awoke in the wee hours of the morning to the sound of rain pelting the window. The same window she'd sat by the night before, peeking around the drawn curtains, overlooking the party that was going on next door. Even across the wide lawn that separated the two houses, she could see the happy people drifting around the pool, could hear the laughter and conversation, although she couldn't make out what they were saying.

She'd scooted to the edge of her bed and lifted herself off into the wheelchair, rolled over to the light switch to flip it off, then waited at the window. Soon after that, she'd seen Scott drive up with Natalie, who looked as frumpy as usual. That girl had absolutely no sense of style! But Scott obviously didn't care. *Natalie has* inner *beauty—the kind that counts!* Katlyn thought sarcastically.

What kind of magic did Natalie have anyway? Even Cissy's friends seemed to like her, chatting and joking as if she were an old friend. Katlyn felt a heavy weight settle in her chest. *I used to be one of them!*

She'd been sitting there, feeling sorry for herself, when Birget had come in to check on her. Then she'd sobbed herself to sleep in the nurse's strong arms, sniffing—in between sobs—the delicate scent Birget always wore.

But Katlyn hadn't slept well; her leg had hurt most of the night. Suppose infection had set in again? Would the doctors even know before it was too late? All kinds of nightmarish possibilities chased through her mind. Katlyn had never really believed she might never walk again—but now, a cold fear gripped her, choking the breath out of her.

This morning, even the sky seemed to be crying with her, the rain rolling like tears down the window-panes. She couldn't eat, didn't speak—not even when her dad stopped by her room to coax her to try an English muffin and some strawberry preserves. After he left for work, her mom came in, but Katlyn still didn't feel like talking. Nothing interested her—not TV, not her favorite CD, nothing. She lay back and sulked.

Only after Cissy called about midmorning and

asked if she could come over did Katlyn's spirits lift a little. She'd already taken her sponge bath. But now she called Birget in to bring her makeup and help her arrange her hair to cover the red scars on her face.

When Cissy arrived, her blue silk shirt spattered with raindrops, she pulled up a chair and crossed her legs. Katlyn hadn't really noticed before, but Cissy had great legs, set off by her white shorts. *Something* I'll *never wear again,* she groaned inwardly. She felt a sting behind her eyes. Why couldn't she turn off the tears this morning?

"Sorry you didn't feel like coming last night, Kat," Cissy began. "But I've got a surprise for you." She brought her hand from behind her back. "Dad made a videotape of the play. So you didn't miss anything, after all!"

Katlyn straightened. "Hey, Birget, can you come in here and crank up my bed?" she called into the room across the hall.

The heavy woman lumbered in right away, operated the electric lever that raised the head of the bed, and propped up Katlyn's pillows. She was about to leave when Cissy stopped her.

"Please don't go. I really owe my success to you. Don't you want to see how well you taught me your Swedish accent?"

"Oh, jah, I'd love to . . ." she began, but halted at the look on Katlyn's face. "But I have vork to do."

Katlyn saw that Cissy seemed disappointed. "It's okay, Birget. Stay . . . if you want to."

As the tape rolled, Katlyn couldn't help laughing at Cissy's antics. "I didn't know you were such a comic!"

Birget's ample bosom was shaking, then she burst out in a roar. "The hand movements—they chust right. And the accent"—she joined her thumb and forefinger—"I couldn't haff done it better my own self."

When it was over, Katlyn was limp with laughter. It felt *won*derful. She hadn't felt this good since before the accident. "Thanks, Cissy. I guess I ended up having the best seat in the house."

Birget wiped the tears from her eyes and excused herself, chuckling all the way back into her room.

With Katlyn more relaxed and happier than she'd seen her in quite a while, Cissy decided to show her the letter. But when Katlyn read it, Cissy wasn't too sure she'd done the right thing. The girl's mouth dropped open, and her face was pale beneath the makeup.

"Th-this is great, Cissy . . . but I thought you said you didn't want to be a professional model anymore."

"I didn't. But this is something left over from my old life," she explained. "I'd forgotten all about entering this competition until the letter came."

"Then you're not turning it down?"

Cissy felt a twinge of guilt. "I-I'm not sure. What do you think I should do?"

Katlyn dropped her eyes to the letter lying in her lap. "An all-expense-paid trip to New York City, a $500 shopping spree, a chance at modeling with a major agency." She glanced up. "Why wouldn't you do it?"

"I've . . . got to be sure it's okay with you first. It's really important to me, Katlyn, that you not question my commitment to God. But I could understand if you did. Here I am—saying one thing, then thinking about running off to New York to flaunt"—she laced her fingers beneath her chin and used her new accent—"my pret-ty face!"

"I'd do it in a heartbeat . . . if I *had* a pretty face," Katlyn pouted.

"But you still do. Your scars are almost gone. I wouldn't even notice them if I didn't know where they were."

"Yeah. I just look naturally lined and wrinkled."

Cissy sighed. "I haven't made a decision, Katlyn. Would you feel better if I didn't go?"

Katlyn seemed to be struggling with an answer. Finally she came out with one. "Well . . . it didn't do much good when Scott shaved his head," she admitted sheepishly.

Gazes locking, they grinned at each other. Then Cissy reached for the letter, refolded it, and crammed it back into her pocket. "I'd really like to do this, Kat. But I hope you believe me when I say I don't want people to view me as just another pretty face or a 'dumb blonde.' I want God's Spirit to shine through . . . *wherever* I go." She fingered the pendant at her neck.

Katlyn shrugged. "Well, *something's* different, that's for sure—ever since the tornado."

"I know God was with me that night. But when Ron ran away, I'd never felt so abandoned in my life—just like you must feel sometimes."

Katlyn nodded. "I'd feel worse if you turned down this chance because of me." She forced a smile. "You'll probably win first place and be in all the magazines."

"Oh, I doubt that. There's a lot of competition out there."

Birget popped her head back in the door. "Will your guest be staying for lunch?"

Cissy jumped up. "Oh, is it lunchtime? I didn't mean to stay this long. I've really got to run. But thanks for all your help with the play. See you later, Kat."

Birget's broad face was all smiles as Cissy bounded out of the room, closing the door behind her.

But Katlyn was steaming. *No! I don't want you to go to New York, Cissy Stiles! It's not fair! It's totally not fair!*

With more strength than she thought she could muster, Katlyn lifted herself out of bed and into the wheelchair, then rolled herself over to the dressing table. Jerking a tissue from its holder, she swiped at her face, rubbing hard to remove the makeup. They were there! Every scar! Every scratch! Inspecting herself closely in the mirror, she examined the great red streaks on her head where the hair was growing back.

She took a hand mirror and, turning, looked at the back of her head. That was the worst of the lot. *I'm still ugly. I'll never be beautiful again. I hate the way I look!*

"I hate *me*!" she screamed at her reflection, resting her forehead in one hand and beating on the table with her fist. "I HATE ME!"

After a long while, she lifted her head and stared at her image. She saw the wild hair, the puffy, red eyes, the pale face. "It's like Daddy said, I'm marred forever. Nothing will ever be the same." She felt as if another brick had been piled on the wall that daily seemed to be separating her from the life she'd had before the accident. How could she get through this? When would it ever stop hurting?

She lowered her eyes to the table and her gaze fell on the little white dove Natalie had given her. Natalie—the perfect Christian, the girl with all the answers, *the girl Scott liked!* And now Cissy—beautiful Cissy, with tons of talent and gorgeous legs to carry her wherever she wanted to go—*she* believed all that stuff Natalie spouted, too.

Katlyn picked up the dove and held it in her palm, stared at it for a long time, then calmly rolled a few feet away. Holding the pin between her thumb and forefinger, she deliberately dropped it into her trash can, out of sight.

Ten

"Helen Lambert spoke at the Women's Club today, Katlyn," Gina Chander confessed one day after the physical therapist had left. "We talked afterward."

Her mom looked especially nice, Katlyn had to admit, in a bright floral print that set off her dark hair. But Katlyn was furious with her. She laid down the book she was reading and glared at her mother. "You know what Daddy said—"

"I know, honey. It isn't often I disagree with your father, but Helen and I go way back. We grew up together in this town before she moved away after marrying Lawrence. She's so distressed over what happened. And as hard as this is for us to bear, I'm almost convinced it would be worse if you were the villain instead of the victim."

Katlyn couldn't believe what she was hearing. "You actually expect me to feel sorry for *them*, Mom?"

"Well . . . I doubt if that's very realistic at this point. But *you* have every possibility of getting well, Katlyn, and Zac is facing jail time and a permanent criminal record. Their whole family is suffering."

"Ha! I wouldn't say they're suffering very much,"

Katlyn snapped, thinking of the party after Cissy's play. All that holier-than-thou talk hadn't changed a thing—not really. All of them were still running around having fun, doing all the summer things she'd like to be doing.

"I hope you'll understand, Katlyn, but I feel so much better since I've talked to Helen. Oh, I know we can't associate with the Lamberts without your father's consent, and he's not likely to give it any time soon. He's still pretty angry about the whole thing—as angry as *you* are." Her mother's level gaze bored a hole right through her. "I really wish you could . . . forgive Zac, honey."

"Forgive?! How can you ask me to do that? You're on *their* side—my own mother!"

"Oh, honey, I'd be on your side even if you'd been the one who had lost control of your car and run into someone else."

Katlyn cringed. She *could* have been. After all, she'd been drinking, too. Not that her mother would ever hear *that* little tidbit—unless Jennifer told. . . .

"It's your anger . . . and bitterness . . . that worry me most, Katlyn. I don't think your legs are going to heal very fast until you find some peace . . . some-where."

Katlyn narrowed her gaze. "That sounds like something Lorna Nolan would say. Have you been talking to my shrink?"

Her mother looked trapped. "Well, yes. And Helen thought—"

"Oh, spare me!" Katlyn turned over, her words muffled by the pillow. "I couldn't care less what any of the *Lamberts* think!"

"You might be surprised," Gina went on. "She had some pretty good ideas. You may very well like at least one of her suggestions."

Katlyn lifted her head, turned back over, and dragged herself up on the pillows again. If she pretended to listen, maybe her mother would go away and leave her alone.

Her mom seemed to fall for that and pulled up a chair, chattering away. "Helen thought you might be willing to see Stephanie and Andy Kelly—they're the youth directors at the church where Helen's sister, Martha Brysen, attends. You know, the young couple who started that new program that's helped so many people since the tornado. White Dove, I think they call it."

White Dove again! Katlyn couldn't escape. It was like that little bird had made a permanent nest in her hair—or what was left of it!

"And since you haven't been very active in *our* church lately, honey . . . well, I thought maybe you'd see them. . . ." Her mother's voice trailed off uncomfortably.

Katlyn started to say no—emphatically, undeniably—no way! But she was curious. Just how many people were actually on Zac's side? If her own mother . . . She shook off the thought.

"Okay, bring them on." She'd find out for herself what everyone was thinking. Besides, it didn't matter anyway. It wouldn't change anything. She was doomed to be a crippled old maid, stuck in a wheelchair for the rest of her life!

Stephanie and Andy Kelly seemed nice enough when they dropped by later in the day, but it wasn't until Stephanie mentioned a car accident when she was seventeen that Katlyn really tuned in.

"Was it a drunk driver?"

"No. It was a head-on collision when a speeding car tried to pass another car approaching from the other lane. My uncle was killed, and I had several broken bones. The worst was my face. The bone in my nose was pushed up into my forehead."

Katlyn stared at the smooth skin. "It doesn't show." In fact, Stephanie was kind of pretty—for an older woman. She had to be at least twenty-something!

Stephanie smiled. "I looked pretty bad for a long time, and I couldn't understand it because I'd given my life to God, and it just didn't seem fair."

Ha! So bad things happened to *good* people, too! Then what was all the fuss about having God in your life anyway if He couldn't even protect His own?

"Did you blame the guy who hit you?"

Stephanie shook her head. "No . . . I didn't."

"Why not?"

After a moment, Stephanie said softly, "The driver was a young woman on her way home from a bridal shower—*hers*. She was killed instantly."

"Whew. That was a bummer." Katlyn couldn't help feeling sorry for the bride-to-be who hadn't lived to see her wedding day. Maybe that's why people were feeling sorry for Zac. He'd definitely caused the problem, but a criminal record might ruin his chances of going to medical school. . . .

"But you said she was speeding. She broke the law,

and she paid for it. So what are you trying to tell me? That Zac should pay for this?" She gestured toward her casts, elevated at the foot of the bed.

"We all pay for our sins, Katlyn."

"*I* didn't do anything! It wasn't *my* fault Zac ran into me. I was standing on the curb, minding my own business!" Katlyn blurted, feeling that awful tightness in her chest again. It was always the same—everyone taking Zac's side—acting like she was to blame somehow.

"I'm not saying you did anything wrong, Katlyn. Sometimes we're victims just because of sin in the world. Life gets messed up for a lot of reasons—our own sinful natures, Satan's influence. But whatever happens, we can feel a certain kind of joy if we give our lives—the whole package, troubles, too—to Jesus. A lot of people have been better witnesses for the Lord while lying in a sickbed than they ever were walking on their own two feet."

"Well, I'm not one of them. I don't deserve this."

"No, you don't, Katlyn," Andy agreed. "No one deserves to be run over by a drunk driver. No one should suffer because of another person's carelessness or sinful actions."

Really? She eyed the good-looking youth director. At least maybe *he* understood.

"Jesus didn't deserve to die either, you know. He didn't deserve to be a victim of the Roman government and His own rebellious people. And we don't deserve heaven or eternal life with God. But that's what He offers us if we give our lives to Him."

"I've gone to church all my life," Katlyn snapped. "I know all that."

113

"I'm sure you do, Katlyn," Stephanie said sweetly. "I did, too, when I lay in bed, wondering if there really was a God. I hoped there was so I could blame Him."

"So what did you do?"

"I tried to say what Jesus said on the cross to the very guys who had put Him there: 'Father, forgive them. They don't know what they're doing.'"

"He forgave those murderers," Andy put in. "And, Katlyn"—he caught her eye, holding the gaze—"He'll forgive Zac . . . if he asks."

She should have known. "Then you think he should get by with this?"

"Not at all," Andy said quickly. "We have to suffer the consequences of our actions here on this earth. But with God's forgiveness, we don't have to suffer eternal consequences. God's forgiving Zac if he repents doesn't mean he shouldn't pay for his crime. He can be a forgiven prisoner. He can make the best of the time he'll have to spend behind bars . . . if that's his sentence."

"Well, now you've told me what God will do for Zac. What about me? *I'm* the one with the broken legs that may never heal. And even if they do, it won't happen before school starts. Can you imagine starting your senior year in a wheelchair!"

Katlyn saw the quick smile of sympathy the Kellys exchanged.

"Katlyn, I want you to think about something," Stephanie put in. "I don't think you know how much you're worth to God. How much He loves you—the real you—the one inside."

Katlyn felt herself retreating. That "inside" talk again!

"You were worth so much to God that 2000 years ago, He proved His love by sending Jesus to the cross to die . . . for my sins, Stephanie's sins, everyone's sins . . . including yours."

"And Zac's," Katlyn added blandly, feeling strangely irritated.

"Zac's too."

"But why would God want me to be crippled?"

"We don't have all the answers to why things happen as they do, Katlyn. But we know the One who does. Maybe God saved your life for a reason. Some are calling it a miracle that you weren't hurt worse."

"Hmph! I'm wondering why He allowed me to get hurt at all!"

The Kellys got real quiet. She'd finally stopped them. They sure couldn't come up with a reason for this one!

Finally, Stephanie spoke up again. "Just imagine how it would be if no one could feel anything. No pain. No joy. No happiness. We'd all be zombies . . . or robots, programmed to respond. What kind of life would that be? But God has given us rules to live by, and when we break them, we hurt ourselves . . . and sometimes others, too."

"Here. Take this." Andy held out a little white dove emblem like Natalie had given Katlyn. The one that was at the bottom of her trash can right now.

Katlyn was so tired of this whole thing. Too tired to argue. Too tired to refuse.

"When you're feeling down—about yourself or someone else—let this remind you of God's Spirit. The Spirit is always around to help you, even if you don't understand."

Katlyn nodded. She was sorry that Stephanie had been hurt. But noses could be rebuilt. Crushed legs, with severed nerves, were a different matter. Stephanie hadn't been faced with possibly living in a wheelchair for the rest of her life.

After they left, Katlyn looked at the tiny pin and was tempted to toss it into the trash along with the other one. But what good would it do? Those birds were everywhere—flocks of them! On T-shirts, on get-well cards, even in the paper and on TV. She dropped the dove onto the table beside the bed. She'd take a nap. Maybe when she woke up, it would have flown away!

But when Katlyn woke up, the dove was still there, daring her to do anything about it.

Her mother popped in a minute later. "I didn't want to disturb you while you were sleeping, honey, but I never told you Helen Lambert's other suggestion."

Katlyn rolled her eyes. It couldn't be any worse than the first one. "What is it?"

"Well, Helen thought—your physical therapist, too—that you might want to do your therapy in the new rehab wing of the hospital. She says it's a lovely place with the latest high-tech equipment. It might do you a world of good to get out a little, Katlyn—see some other people for a change."

"That's exactly what I *don't* want to do, *Mother*. At least, I don't want people to see *me*."

Gina Chander brightened. What was her mom up to? "That's the best part, darling. You can schedule your visits any time you want. With the flexible working hours these days, some therapists prefer to work at night. So you could be there when there are fewer people around. But at least you'd have a change of scenery."

Change of scenery. Maybe that's exactly what Katlyn needed.

Still, when she reached Garden City General a little after eight o'clock, Katlyn couldn't believe she'd let her parents talk her into this. Birget had driven her in a van her dad had rented, wheeled her into the contemporary new wing of the hospital, then disappeared to find "an old friend" at the nurse's station on another floor.

The sharp-looking woman in exercise gear sitting at the desk came around to sign her in. "I'm Terri. Am I glad to see you! This place has been dead all night. I'll welcome the company, Katlyn."

"How did you know my name?"

"Well, Dr. Lambert called to tell us to be expecting you. You're Katlyn Chander, aren't you?"

So much for anonymity! The Lamberts, again. "Yeah, that's me," she all but snarled. "Let's get this over with."

The woman had the nerve to laugh. "Oh, don't be so grim. It's not that bad. In fact, we're pretty proud of what we accomplish here."

She stepped behind the chair and wheeled Katlyn through a pair of wide doors that opened automatically—like the doors of the supermarket! For a minute, Katlyn almost panicked, flashing back to that awful night.

"In here in the main room, you'll find all the machines you'll be using to strengthen upper-body muscles and torso while your legs heal. This one"—she pointed to a sleek model—"is the Uppercycle. It's something like a bicycle without wheels."

"How do you expect me to ride that thing?"

"Oh, you don't even have to leave your chair. You simply roll into position, grab the handles, and pump your arms instead of your legs. This little panel gives you a readout of how you're doing. It's all computerized."

Terri wheeled Katlyn around the room, explaining the various pieces of equipment and the cubicles where she would later be receiving electrical stimulation to the nerve endings in her legs.

"Sounds like something out of *Frankenstein's Bride*," grumbled Katlyn.

"You'll get used to it. Some people don't feel much more than a tingle."

From behind them came a whooshing sound as the doors opened, and Katlyn turned to see another wheelchair—this one manned by a one-legged child with a snaggle-toothed grin. She gasped. *That could have been me! Might still be. . . .*

"Hi, Miss Terri." The little boy sounded like a bullfrog. The deep voice seemed too big for his body. "Where's my buddy?"

Terri glanced at her watch. "Oh, he'll be here any minute. Why don't you just go ahead and change into your swim trunks?"

"I've already got 'em on—under here!" With that, he flashed another smile and rolled his chair toward the double doors on one side of the room as fast as his scrawny arms would churn.

Terri must have been a mind reader, Katlyn thought, because she answered Katlyn's questions before she had a chance to ask. "Chad's one of our favorites around here. Sad story, though. So we try to give him as much love and attention as possible. He's all through with chemo—for a while—and since there's no one—at least, no reliable person—at home to look after him, we bend the rules a little and allow him to swim here at night. He's struck up quite a friendship with . . ." She gave Katlyn a peculiar look, then went on. ". . . an older guy who comes around a lot. He's not even a volunteer—just a friend."

Katlyn glanced back at the doors leading to the reception area. But no more small tornados roared through. How could anyone with only one leg be so cheerful?

"Let's finish our tour," Terri went on. "Then we'll check on Chad until his partner gets here." She seemed a little nervous, Katlyn thought as they rolled on to the next piece of equipment.

"Now *this* is one of our newer marvels. While a patient is doing dull reps—treadmill, upper-body workouts, that kind of thing—we combine the physical therapy with mood music"—Terri indicated several sets of earphones, then pressed a button on a wall panel—"and instant vacations!"

Before Katlyn's eyes, the blank wall was transformed into a tropical beach, sparkling blue water lapping against diamond white sand. "Wow! That looks like the place where we spent a month last summer."

In the very next instant, she felt that familiar sinking sensation—like descending in an express elevator. She might *never* water-ski or snorkel again.

Terri hurried to press another button. "Or maybe you'd prefer a hike along a mountain trail."

"You've got to be kidding! In *this* thing?"

"Consider this an incentive, Katlyn. It's—"

Terri turned when the doors whooshed open again. "Chad's already here," she called to someone. "He's probably waiting for you beside the pool."

By the time Katlyn could maneuver her chair to find out who had come in, all she could see was his back, disappearing through the doors on the opposite wall. Whoever it was, though, had on one of those White Dove T-shirts. Could it be Scott? But what would Scott be doing here?

"Let's move on to the pool area," Terri suggested. "You can at least tour the facility. Sooner or later, you'll be doing some water therapy yourself. And you can see how much progress Chad is making. He swims like a fish now."

Katlyn couldn't bear the thought. If she ever did lose her leg, she'd never be caught *dead* in a swimsuit again!

Terri steered her through the wide doors and was halfway through a covered walkway when they heard shouts. Speeding the rest of the way, they came to a tiled floor surrounding a huge pool, covered by a glass bubble. Reflecting back from above, the pool lights twinkled like stars.

But Katlyn registered nothing more. Bending over the little boy she had seen earlier and administering

CPR was a familiar form. His drenched shirt and shorts clung to his muscular frame; his hair was plastered to his skull. Pausing between breaths, he looked up and his eyes locked with hers. Not brown eyes like Scott's—but *blue*!

Zac Lambert!

But there was no time to think. No time to feel.

"Take over for a minute, will you, Terri?" Zac gasped.

"Wh-what happened?" Katlyn whispered.

Zac unfolded his long legs from a crouch and straightened. "He was in the pool when I got here—face down. All I can figure is that he must have gotten a leg cramp."

Terri moved aside to catch her breath, and Zac took her place, pinching the little boy's nostrils shut and breathing into his mouth. "The poor little guy must have gotten tired of waiting for Zac. I should *never* have let him out of my sight!" she moaned.

There was a gurgling sound, and water spewed out of Chad's mouth. The next minute he was coughing up his lungs. He sat up, looking around as if he was still in a daze. Then, seeing Zac, he smiled a watery smile. "I didn't think you'd *ever* come!"

"Hey there, champ. Welcome back." Katlyn watched as big, tall Zac dropped to his knees and cuddled the little boy in his arms, looking pretty watery himself. She hadn't seen many guys cry—but then it wasn't every day one saved someone's life . . .

. . . or ruined someone else's! She clenched her jaw. Zac Lambert might be a hero right this minute. But as far as she was concerned, he was still the jerk who had robbed her of what could have been the best summer of her life!

Eleven

"I'm scared," Katlyn admitted to Jennifer the morning of the trial, forcing out of her mind the tender scene with Zac and the little boy at the rehab pool. "What do you think Zac will say?"

Her sister spread her hands. "What *can* he say— except that he's sorry? But it's no more than he's been trying to tell you for several weeks now. He's admitted he ran into you. He's sent all those cards and letters you won't open, even flowers. The guy really seems sincere, Kat."

Katlyn nodded. She remembered the night little Chad had nearly drowned. Zac had tried to talk to her then, too. But of *course* he was sorry. Weren't people always sorry when they were about to go to jail? She was plenty sorry, too, but it hadn't changed the facts.

She shot Jennifer a worried look. "Suppose he tells the judge there was drinking at the party?"

"Why should he?"

"To save his skin, of course!" Katlyn interrupted. "To get a lighter sentence. If he mentions that other people were drinking, too—that there was liquor in *our* bar . . .

"I've had a lot of time on my hands, so I've been watching trials on TV. Defense attorneys come up with a lot of tricks. I mean, they bring out all sorts of things . . . about people. I'm just afraid they'll twist things."

Jennifer sighed. "I'm over twenty-one, Katlyn. I'm old enough to drink. And some of the others at the party were, too."

"Yeah, but you see how Dad feels about Zac's whole family. He's been blaming all of them for what happened to me. He might even blame you for letting the gang help themselves that night."

"Look, I didn't make anyone do *any*thing. Dad knows I couldn't force Zac to drink. He's responsible for his own actions."

"Suppose Scott or Natalie or Cissy bring it up? They know Zac was drinking at our lake house. That's why they wanted him to leave." Katlyn glanced at the white dove on her nightstand. "You know *they'll* tell the whole truth."

"I wish you'd let me talk to Dad. He'd know what to do."

"No!" Katlyn's eyes were wild. "Please, Jen! You promised!"

"Well . . . it's against my better judgment. But you're right. I *did* promise. Just think about it and let me know if you change your mind. It would sure clear my conscience."

After Jennifer left the room, Katlyn swung her legs over the side of the bed and hoisted herself into the wheelchair. Those upper-body workouts she'd been getting at the Rehab Center *did* seem to be helping, she had to admit. She pressed the button that triggered the motor on her chair and moved to the dressing table.

She didn't look too bad, she decided. But she didn't look too good either. She hadn't slept much at all, and there were dark circles under her eyes. She was thinner, too. But at least her bald spots were covered, and the rest of her hair was still thick and shiny.

Leaning closer to the mirror, Katlyn inspected her face. The scars were fading, but so was her tan. She looked pale—actually pretty ghastly. And her lips—once soft and full—seemed to have thinned into a tight line.

"You look like you haven't slept a wink all night," her father observed when he and her mom came in to bring her breakfast. "Good. Don't change a thing. No makeup, no special hairdo."

"Chan!" Gina exclaimed. "How heartless!"

"Daddy, I—"

He didn't wait to hear what Katlyn had to say. "This is just the look we want for the trial. I want the judge to see every scar, every scratch. I want him to know what that boy has done to you!" The curl of her father's lip looked like a carbon copy of her own.

"I still don't think she should go," Katlyn's mom said with a worried frown.

"Gina"—he gave a frustrated sigh, the kind some people use with very small children—"you know as well as I do that the doctors have given their permission. We've rented that van with a bed in back, and Miss Birget will be right beside her. We *need* Katlyn. She's our star witness."

Katlyn felt weird. Had she been watching too many lawyer shows on TV? This whole thing was beginning to sound like something out of *Law and Order* or one of those old *Perry Mason* episodes.

She felt her lip trembling and bit down. She hated to go out in public looking like this. Everyone would be there. But Daddy said it had to be done. And she was the only one to do it.

The scars were definitely healing. And she could always use makeup to cover what was left—at least, any other day. But what about her legs? The nerves had not healed yet. What if they never did? There was deep inner scarring, the doctors had said. And it would take time, a lot of time . . . with the constant possibility of re-infection.

That's what she had to remember, Katlyn thought, feeling mad and determined again. And she had to convince the judge, too. Zac Lambert was guilty and deserved to be punished. It wouldn't be fair if she turned out to be the *only* one who had to serve out a sentence—imprisoned by a wheelchair for the rest of her life!

Zac was standing with his parents and their attorney near a huge, white column on the porch of the courthouse in Oakwood when the Chanders drove up. The car was closely followed by a big van. Zac tuned out the conversation around him. He was more interested in the action straight ahead.

He watched as Katlyn's parents got out of the Cadillac, trailed by Jennifer, who had been sitting in the backseat. Then a big woman in a nurse's uniform emerged from the driver's side of the van and proceeded to go around back, where she opened the door. Zac couldn't help thinking that all of the principle players in the cast were accounted for now—all, that is, except one.

All eyes were trained on the rear door of the van. Rolling down a ramp that had unfolded at the touch of a control was Katlyn, sitting in her wheelchair and looking pretty pathetic. What judge wouldn't be moved? Zac had about as much chance of beating this as a snowflake in July!

It would have been funny if it hadn't been so horrible, Zac thought, seeing the Chanders and the Lamberts face off like gunfighters at the O.K. Corral. But he'd better not show a trace of a smile. That could be interpreted as taking the situation lightly, their attorney had warned. Well, Zac didn't want them to see his tears either. He choked them back, wondering who he felt sorrier for today—himself or Katlyn Chander.

He didn't want to go to jail. Yet he was sure she didn't like the idea of being a cripple . . . for maybe longer than that. One minute, Zac felt like fleeing the scene—like a fugitive from justice. The next, he was ready to take his medicine "like a man." There was one sure thing—nothing he could offer could undo the damage he'd done Katlyn Chander. If they threw the book at him . . . well, he deserved it.

Zac snapped back to the present when his attorney voiced what he'd been thinking: "I just hope they don't put that girl on the stand."

But "that girl" was here now, her dad pushing her wheelchair toward the concrete ramp at the side of the steps. There was no avoiding them. Mrs. Chander nodded slightly and turned her head. Neither Katlyn nor Jennifer would look his way. But Mr. Chander's long, level stare slashed him like a knife.

I'm sunk, Zac moaned inwardly.

He'd asked God to forgive him. Katlyn, too—in all those letters that had been returned unopened. He'd learned a lot in the past few weeks—about how a substance could alter a mind until it couldn't function responsibly. How alcohol could take over a person's life. How a habit could become a disease. Yeah, he'd learned a lot. Too late.

Today a judge would decide his future. His prominent parents couldn't help him now. His Aunt Martha, a very influential woman, could only speak up about his past character. But it wouldn't make any difference. That young girl in the wheelchair spoke louder than words.

Zac tugged at his tie, adjusted his sportcoat, and tried to square his shoulders as he entered the courtroom. *Now it's payday!*

The judge was already seated at the bench hearing cases. Zac felt his spirits droop further as, one by one, the offenders were handed what seemed pretty tough judgments, along with a tongue-lashing. The stern-faced man, whose name plate read Judge Oliver Hayes, apparently had no sympathy for defendants.

Taking a minute to glance around the courtroom, Zac noticed some of the high school crowd sitting together near the back. He recognized several guys who played on the basketball team at Shawnee High; that funny, redheaded girl who hung out with Natalie Ainsworth, Scott's friend; and Natalie, of course. She'd be here to support Scott. But what about the others? He figured some of them must be Katlyn's friends.

Just for a flash, Zac recalled that Natalie's dad was supposed to be some kind of correctional officer at the prison not too far from Garden City. How ironic—if Zac ended up seeing the guy every day for the next year!

His Aunt Martha was here, too, with Cissy and the Stileses, sitting across the aisle from the Chanders' entourage—complete with nurse and counselor. Zac wondered if the families would ever be friends again. Just look what a few drinks had done—pretty nearly divided a whole town!

He shook off the disturbing thought and tuned in to was what going on around him. The bailiff was calling the case of Chander vs. Lambert.

"How does the defendant plead?" the judge asked.

"Guilty, your honor," came the reply from the prosecuting attorney.

"Is that correct?" Judge Hayes addressed Zac's defense attorney, a youngish guy in a conservative suit and tie. Zac couldn't help thinking he was wearing just the thing for a funeral—*Zac's*!

"Yes, your honor. Since this is Mr. Lambert's first offense, we're asking the leniency of the court."

"On what basis?"

"The defendant has just completed his sophomore year of college with outstanding grades and has been an exemplary young man until this unfortunate incident took place, your honor. We have witnesses who will testify to his high moral character."

Zac's attorney took his seat, and Judge Hayes turned to the prosecuting attorney. "How does your client feel about this?"

"Because of the severity of the injuries sustained by my client—possible permanent damage to both legs, thus crippling her for life—*and*"—he turned a stern gaze on Zac, who felt himself quaking in his shoes—"because the defendant has already admitted to driving under the influence, we are requesting the maximum sentence, your honor—definite jail time. Whatever financial remuneration this court awards will not be enough to reimburse Miss Chander for emotional and psychological damages, but we are asking for all that the law allows."

"Will the defendant rise?"

Zac stood shakily, bracing his legs against the table in front of him.

"Mr. Lambert, are you aware of the charges which have been brought against you?"

He cleared his throat, hoping his voice wouldn't crack. "Yes, your honor."

"Has anyone coerced you, forced you in any way to plead guilty to these charges?"

"No, your honor."

"This is your plea, from your own free will."

"Yes, sir . . . your honor."

"Do you understand that, with the plea of guilty, you are forever barred from appeal?"

"Yes, I am . . . uh . . . I *do*."

"Do you realize that I am under no obligation to take your attorney's recommendation for leniency? That I can sentence you to 364 days, plus a fine?"

"Yes."

"Then, with those things in mind, how do you plead?"

Zac took a deep breath, the events of the night of the accident flashing through his brain at a speed faster than sound. This was it. Once the plea was officially received by the judge, he couldn't go back on it. But it wouldn't matter. Everyone knew he was guilty. To plead innocent would only ensure the maximum sentence. "I am . . . guilty, your honor."

His attorney had told him to say nothing more. There would be time for him to speak later—if it would do any good.

"How old are you, son?"

"Nineteen, sir."

"Nineteen." The judge was nodding, Zac noticed, probably thinking he was old enough to know better. "Nineteen years old and facing a jail sentence because of foolishness, lack of control. And you ask me for leniency? Can you give me one good reason why you deserve leniency?"

Zac could no longer meet the judge's stern gaze. He swallowed hard and shook his head.

"I can't *hear* you." Right now, his honor sounded like a drill sergeant, Zac thought.

Zac forced the words past his lips. "No, sir." Everyone knew he didn't deserve leniency. And this judge sure wasn't the type to grant any.

Zac felt a movement beside him and turned to see his attorney standing to his feet. "*I* can, your honor."

The judge glared over his glasses. "I'm not asking you." The attorney sat down.

"Do you know how many people are killed each year because of drinking and driving?"

"I-I've been doing a lot of reading, sir, and going to meetings—"

The judge didn't let him finish. "Where did you get your liquor, son?"

Zac looked down, hoping the black-robed judge would let him off the hook on this one.

But he pressed on. "No answer? Are you defying this court? I can hold you in contempt, you know, young man."

"Yes, sir . . . no, sir. I'm sorry, your honor."

"Sorry? That's all you have to say? Did you steal the liquor? Did someone give it to you? Did you lie about your age?"

Zac's head swam.

"I'll ask you one more time, son. Where did you get the liquor?"

Zac shook his head and let the tears rain down his face.

The judge picked up his gavel.

"No! Wait, your honor!" Helen Lambert, a trail of watery mascara streaking down her cheeks, approached the bench. The defense attorney stood to intercept her. "Please, may I speak?"

"Identify yourself."

"Helen Lambert, sir, Zac's mother," she began. "My son is not being belligerent, your honor. He's trying to protect *me*. I'm an alcoholic. He got into a bottle I had hidden in our lake house. It's my fault. I've given my family such a terrible time for so long. It all came to a turning point the night of the accident. I realized for the first time how I've hurt my family, how much pain I've caused my boys. . . ."

There was a pause before she continued. "Oh, I know Zac is guilty of the charge against him. And I know he has to pay. But please don't blame him for trying to protect me."

The judge didn't try to intervene when she turned toward Zac. "Oh, son, don't worry about me. I've gone public with my problem. Please, just tell the judge you got the liquor from my hidden supply." She faced the judge again. "You see, I'm guilty, too. For not being a better mother . . . for keeping alcohol in my home around my growing sons. If I'd admitted I was an alcoholic much earlier, I might have been able to prevent what happened. But I didn't. So I'm asking, your honor, if there's a way . . . let me pay for this crime, too. Let me take part of my son's sentence!"

Zac was sobbing out loud, hands over his face. "Mom, don't do this," he choked out. "I'm the one to blame here, not you. I don't want that on my conscience, too."

"Order, order in the court!" Judge Hayes demanded. "Get a hold of yourself, son. And please be seated, Mrs. Lambert." As soon as she had been escorted back to sit with her family, the judge addressed Zac. "Mr. Lambert, face the victim."

Zac turned slowly. Mr. Chander's fists were clenched. Mrs. Chander and Jennifer were crying. Sitting in the wheelchair rolled out in the aisle beside her parents, Katlyn looked as if she'd been run over by a train instead of a small sports car—useless legs propped out in front of her, dark eyes huge in her white face, a few wisps of hair sprouting from the shaved areas on her head like a scarecrow's.

Zac hated the sting of hot moisture behind his eyelids. Hated the heat creeping up the back of his neck. The sticky sweat in the palms of his hands. The weakness in his knees. *What a wimp!* He balanced himself with one hand on the table behind him.

"I'm sorry," he rasped, hating most of all how his voice sounded. "I'm . . . really sorry."

"Sorry for what you did to my daughter—or sorry you're going to jail!" grated Mr. Chander.

"Both." He might as well be honest. "I'm sorry I hurt Katlyn. Sorry I hurt your family. I don't know why I did it. I've had a few sessions with a Christian counselor. And I've been going to meetings . . . trying to figure it all out. They think it may be because—" he cringed as he glanced in his mom's direction.

"That's no excuse, young man," Chander interrupted impatiently. "No use trying to blame it on someone else!"

"Well, I'm also sorry I'm going to jail. To tell you the truth, I'm scared to death." Zac shifted his feet, feeling clumsy and awkward. "I've been telling myself I ought to face this like a man. But I don't feel much like a man. I feel more like a scared kid who'd really like to crawl up in his mother's lap and cry on her shoulder." He waited while Helen Lambert launched a fresh volley of tears, then quieted down a little.

"Honest, your honor, I thought I could handle this better. But as you can see . . ." He ducked his head. "I'm not doing too well." He looked up, dreading what he'd read on the Chanders' faces. "All I can say is . . . I'm sorry."

Out of the corner of his eye, Zac spotted movement in the back of the courtroom. Filing in and taking a seat at the back were Andy and Stephanie Kelly, and Terri and Joel from the Rehab Center. What in the world were *they* doing here?

As he saw their nods of encouragement, an idea began to form. *Whoa! Is that you, Lord?*

Suddenly Zac knew what he had to do.

Twelve

"I hadn't planned on giving *this* kind of testimony in court," Zac began. "But, with the court's permission . . ." At Judge Hayes's nod, he continued. "I think you need to know what's happened to me *since* the accident." He hesitated as if not sure whether to go on.

"I gave my *heart* to Jesus Christ when I was just a little guy—about the age of someone I met this summer." He caught Terri's eye, and she gave him a wink. "But I didn't give Jesus my *life*. I hung on to it. Wanted to make my own decisions, wanted to be in the driver's seat. Except"—he gave a dry laugh—"I didn't turn out to be such a hot driver. In fact, I blew it in more ways than one.

"I won't go into it all here, but let's just say it has something to do with a white bird, a really cool kid, and a second chance at life. . . ." He waited for the buzz to die down after his strange announcement. "This may not make very much sense to you, but let me just say it makes plenty of sense to me . . . for the first time. God has given me another chance. I hope you can, too."

As Zac sat down, Mr. Chander shot to his feet.

"Now he's hiding behind *religion*, of all things! His cousin here is a pretty convincing little actress. Must run in the family!"

Judge Hayes rapped with his gavel again. "That remark was uncalled for, Mr. Chander. The young man has admitted his guilt and has issued an apology."

"Oh, I can believe he's sorry, all right. Anyone would be sorry to be facing a jail sentence." Mr. Chander's voice rang with conviction. "*I'm* even sorry for him—for the whole family. But I'm sorrier for my daughter—my joyful, carefree daughter—who has been bedridden for weeks and may never walk again. I'm sorry she's had to lose her trust because of this boy's stupid decision!"

Plunging on, Mr. Chander turned toward the Lamberts across the aisle. "These people used to be our friends. But now, I'm not even sure I know them. They're not the family I thought they were. A doctor who can't even diagnose his own wife's illness! A marriage that's evidently so unstable the wife turns to alcohol! And what's going on with this boy who almost kills my daughter? Not to mention the younger brother." All eyes turned toward Scott's nearly bald head. "Is he a skinhead or something?"

At that, Helen Lambert gasped. "You have no idea—"

Dr. Lambert's arm went around her shoulders, and he shook his head as if warning her not to say anything more.

"Stop it! Stop it!" Jennifer screamed on the other side of the aisle, just as Katlyn erupted, "No, Daddy! Scott did that for *me*!"

Mrs. Chander pulled on her husband's sleeve. "Chan, please!"

He jerked away and lunged for Zac, stopped short of punching him in the face by a deputy who grabbed Chander's arm. "I wouldn't try that if I were you, sir."

"Order! Order in this court!" Judge Hayes demanded. "I'll tolerate no further outbursts!"

Chander's chest heaved and set, but finally he relaxed a little and pushed his hand through his thinning hair. "I'm sorry, your honor. But it's been a tough time for all of us. We'd planned a family trip to Europe this summer. But with our daughter's accident . . . well, we've been holding our breath ever since . . . not knowing if she'll be normal again. There's got to be some kind of restitution. We can't let this pass. I don't like this—don't like it at all . . . not speaking to folks who used to be our friends. But I can't let my little girl think I didn't do everything in my power to see that that boy pays for what he's done to her!"

Over his shoulder, Zac watched as the nurse stepped into the aisle and knelt down beside Katlyn, patting her shoulder, while a blond woman leaned over to whisper something in her ear.

"I'm always sorry to see families torn apart this way," the judge said. "It's easy to blame such tragedies as the Chander accident on alcohol. And no question about it—alcohol abuse is a huge problem in our society. But alcohol can do no harm unless someone decides to pick up a drink and swallow it. That's where the responsibility lies."

There was not a sound in the courtroom as the judge went on. "I believe I have a fair understanding of what's going on here. And though I always regret this part of my duties . . . well, it's time to render a decision. Will the defendant please rise?"

Zac scuffed his chair away from the table, barely aware of anything except the thudding of his heart. *Oh, God, please don't let me act like a baby. Don't let me faint. Help me take whatever comes.*

But each blow of the gavel was like a hammer blow to his brain. His head throbbed. His knees wobbled. With the gavel lifted to strike for a final time, all Zac could think was, *What's taking so long? Let's get this over with. . . .*

"Zac Lambert, you have pleaded guilty to the charge of felony DUI. It is my duty to sentence you to—"

"No!"

A gasp went up from the Chanders' side. Jennifer Chander was making her way past her mother and father into the aisle. She shrugged off her dad's attempt to stop her, sailed by Katlyn in the wheelchair, and marched down to the front of the courtroom. "Please, may I say something?" she asked Judge Hayes.

He laid the gavel down with a shake of his head, as if he couldn't believe yet another interruption. "Go ahead, young lady."

Jennifer turned around. "I'm sorry, Katlyn. I know I promised, but I can't live with this on my conscience." She swiveled back to face the judge. "I'm not asking for any favors for Zac, your honor. But I can't keep quiet about this. I never forced anyone to take a drink the night of our party—the same night as the accident—but I did let some of the kids know we had alcohol in our bar."

"Jennifer?" Mr. Chander croaked.

"I'm sorry, Dad, but it's true. I allowed drinking at the party. Zac hadn't had anything to drink until he got to our lake house. But by the time he left, he was noticeably drunk. That part is my fault, Daddy, and I can't let you put all the blame on the Lamberts. I have to live with myself, too." Her words trailed off as she walked back to take a seat two rows behind her family.

Katlyn covered her face with her hands. "You promised," she mumbled. "You promised."

Another whirlwind of activity broke out. The judge banged his gavel. Chander stood, reaching out for Jennifer as she walked past, just as Katlyn wheeled around to face her dad. "Daddy, I can't stand any more of this. I—"

Zac jumped up. "It doesn't matter where I got it! Jennifer and Katlyn gave a nice party, and I ruined everything. I might have had a few drinks while I was there, but when I got home, I drank some more. It's all my fault!"

There was a flurry of motion as everyone began to talk at once, while both attorneys attempted to calm their clients.

The judge continued to bang his gavel. "This is an outrage! You people are very near being held in contempt of court!"

Everyone settled down as the deputies stepped forward, a grim look on their faces.

Over his glasses, the judge speared Zac with a stern eye. "Zac Lambert, I've given very serious thought to your crime, as well as your background, and have taken into consideration that you have no previous record, have made an honest attempt to better understand the effects of alcohol, and have shown remorse for your actions. Therefore, I sentence you to . . ."

Zac's heart nearly stopped beating.

" . . . twenty hours per week community service while on two years probation, suspension of your driver's license for two years, and a $1,000 restitution fine to be paid to the victim within two years at a rate that will be determined."

He banged his gavel one more time, pushed his glasses farther up on his nose, and called, "Next case."

Zac didn't budge. Everyone around him seemed to be moving in slo-mo. What about jail? Had the judge not said anything about *jail*?

"We're outta here," Zac's attorney said close to his ear as he took his arm and steered him toward the door at the rear of the courtroom. "When Chander realizes you've walked, he'll be a raging bull!"

———

Katlyn sobbed in back of the van while Lorna Nolan did her best to console her. But there was nothing anyone could say to make her feel better.

"I've never seen Daddy this mad," Jennifer said on the way home from her seat beside Birget. "He's driving like a maniac."

"Now that is a man who should not have zee license. Anger make accident like alcohol, I think," Birget commented.

"Maybe," Katlyn gulped, "maybe he's trying to catch the Lamberts. And when he does, I'm afraid he'll kill Zac."

"Your father is too wise to do anything like that."

Dr. Nolan's firm words didn't fool Katlyn. "He's furious! With Zac . . . with Jen . . . and if he finds out I was drinking, too, he'll be furious with *me*!" she wailed.

Her dad was still ranting and raving long after they got home. Even her mother stopped trying to reason with him. Katlyn only hoped the Lamberts would steer clear of the Stileses' house and not show up anywhere near her father while he was in this state.

"I'll see what I can do," Lorna Nolan offered but came back to Katlyn's room to say it was like talking to a stone wall. Then, after promising to stay in touch, she left for her office in Oakwood.

Katlyn lay staring at the ceiling until Birget brought her lunch. Before the nurse escaped to her own room across the hall, she smiled cheerfully. "Try to take a little nap. Maybe Daddy will feel better later, jah?"

Fat chance of that, Katlyn thought. The truth was, her daddy was out of control. And wasn't she a prime example of what could happen when another person lost control? She shuddered. Before this thing was over, someone else could be hurt.

Someone had to *do* something! But what? And who?

The air was suddenly stifling, and it was hard to breathe. Even with the air-conditioning on, Katlyn felt herself getting steamy. She glanced at the lunch tray. The lettuce in her sandwich looked about as wilted as she felt. And the ice in her tea had almost melted. She shoved the tray aside. She couldn't possibly eat anything—not with so much eating *her*!

She eased to the side of the bed, pulled the wheel-chair over and slipped into it, then rolled over to look in the mirror. All the tiny streaks and scars on her face showed. They always turned pinker when she was upset. Her hair was matted and wet from tears.

"Ugly!" she whispered, remembering the day she had thrown her mirror across the room and broke it into a zillion pieces. Hearing the sound of breaking glass coming from downstairs, she realized Daddy was doing some of that right now.

Staring at her reflection, her red, puffy eyes, she sighed. Where would it all end? Her family was breaking apart right before her eyes. Mom and Daddy weren't getting along. She and Daddy hadn't talked about anything but revenge for weeks. Only Jennifer seemed to be making any sense at all.

Like father, like daughter, came a little voice. *What did you expect? Aren't you just like your daddy?* How many times had she heard those words? She'd always loved being compared to her father, always loved being "Daddy's little girl." But she wasn't a little girl any longer. And biting sarcasm and temper tantrums weren't very attractive in grown-ups. Was she on the way to being out of control, too?

She wheeled over to the trash can and rummaged through it. It had been emptied. The little dove was gone. Would God think she had thrown *Him* away? She felt panicky—like she'd felt when she'd found out she might lose a leg. But wouldn't it be much worse to lose your soul? The very idea was terrifying.

Wasn't there another one of those doves? *Yes!* She glanced over at her nightstand. But the little pin wasn't there. She pawed through her jewelry box. Here it was! Birget must have put it away.

She took out the white dove, grasping it tightly as if it might fly away. Then she looked in the mirror again, her wild-eyed gaze haunted and strained.

"Oh, God," she said fearfully, "I want to be healed—on the inside."

The tears began again—first a trickle, then a stream. Finally, a flood. She sobbed until there were no tears left, no strength—just a deep quietness. She seemed to remember a Bible verse about God's Spirit being like a river flowing through a person. Could He be washing her clean?

Too exhausted to hold up her head, she leaned it against the dressing table, letting the peace flow over her, around her. Cissy said God had changed her on the inside. Even Scott had shaved his head to prove to her that the outside wasn't so important. Mrs. Lambert had changed. Zac had changed. So maybe she could, too.

But what was the next step? Almost immediately a Bible verse popped into her head—one she'd memorized eons ago, when she was just a little girl in Sunday school: "Our Father, who art in heaven . . . forgive us our trespasses, as we forgive those who trespass against us." She hadn't thought much about it since. She'd never felt the need to forgive anyone. It was different now. Zac had asked her to forgive him, to give him another chance. Now the ball was in her court.

"Please, God. Heal me inside. And help my daddy."

Katlyn lost all track of time. She didn't know how long she had lain there with her head on her arms. Finally she looked up. Had it happened? Had she been forgiven? Had she forgiven Zac? She didn't feel anything. Only emptiness—like a great, big weight had eased off her chest.

With a sigh she rolled into the bathroom, washed her face, and returned to the dressing table where she carefully applied her makeup, using the foundation to conceal her scars the way Cissy had taught her. Then she brushed her hair away from her face, arranging it over the shaved sections, and put on tiny rhinestone earrings. They sort of matched the sparkle in her eyes, she thought, smiling.

Suddenly the reflection in the mirror opened its mouth, forming an O of surprise. Sparkle? Smile? Where had they come from?

She moved over to the window, parted the curtains, and looked up toward heaven, where the white clouds were tumbling in the sky like fleecy sheep. "Thank you," she said aloud. Something was . . . different.

In a playful mood, she wheeled in a circle, then went over to the dresser, picked up the little dove, and rolled across the hall, where she banged on Birget's door.

In a minute, the nurse opened it, looking groggy, her hair all askew. She pushed at it, embarrassed. "Oh, I must have taken zee nap myself. I didn't hear you ring."

"No problem," Katlyn assured her. "I just need some help getting into the chair lift." She cleared her throat and added, "If you wouldn't mind."

She couldn't help laughing at the look on Miss Birget's face. She could almost read her thoughts. Katlyn Chander asking if she *minded*?

After Miss Birget fastened the chair onto the lift, Katlyn waved her off. "Go finish your nap. I can manage now. And . . . thanks."

Leaving Miss Birget staring after her in disbelief, Katlyn found her dad at the bar, with a drink in front of him.

Hearing the hum of the wheelchair, he looked up and narrowed his gaze, as if trying to focus. "Oh, it's you, Princess. You're looking mighty pretty."

"Thank you, Daddy." Maybe he thought so because she looked different with makeup. Or maybe when you're clean on the inside, you look better on the outside. Or maybe . . . it was the drinking that clouded his vision. . . .

"Does that help, Daddy?" she asked carefully, glancing toward the shot glass.

He took a deep breath and fingered the rim. "I just needed a little something to steady my nerves, honey, thash all." She heard the slurred words, saw the muscle flex in his jaw.

"I know," she said softly. "I know just how you feel. That's how I felt, too, until a few minutes ago."

He frowned, blinking. "Wh-what are you talkin' about?"

"I used *this*." She laid the white dove on the counter beside his drink. "I mean, I used what it represents."

He stared, eyes red, at the two objects in front of him—the glass and the dove. "Oh, boy." He swiped at his mouth with the back of his hand, then ran his hand over his neck and hair, leaving it mussed, the sparse hair sticking up in spikes.

Katlyn waited, not knowing what to do next. She knew her daddy had always prided himself on not being overly religious. Would he even understand what she was trying to tell him?

She took a deep breath. "I have a confession," she said and felt her mouth go dry. She swallowed hard. This wasn't going to be as easy as she'd thought. So she blurted it right out. "I was drinking that night, too, Daddy."

His eyes widened. "Don't lie to me, Katlyn. I've let you taste alcohol so you wouldn't have to 'speriment. Said you didn't like the taste."

"I . . . wasn't drinking it for the taste."

He shook his head. "Can't believe . . . Jennifer would let you."

"She didn't, Daddy. She's not my baby-sitter. Besides, we've grown up with alcohol in the house—with the temptation right under our noses." Katlyn stopped herself before she said something that would only rile her father unnecessarily. "Anyway, *I'm* the one who offered Zac a drink. It wasn't Jennifer. I can't let her take the blame."

"I'm not blaming her, Katlyn. She's a big girl. And Zac is a big boy. Nobody *forced* him to take it, did they?"

"No, but I . . . maybe . . . tempted him."

"Oh, come on!" He lifted the glass, took a big gulp, then set it down—hard. Then he slumped over the glass, tousled hair falling over his forehead so she couldn't see his eyes anymore.

Katlyn turned to leave. She could have kicked herself. She'd already blown it . . . and just when she was beginning to think there was some hope. . . .

She wheeled around to see her mother and Jennifer walking into the bar. "Well, I guess you heard me tell Daddy about . . . that night." Katlyn dropped her head. "I might as well finish the story. I was jealous of Natalie—jealous that Scott had invited *her* to the lake . . . that he was at the party with *her* instead of *me*. But I tried to act like I didn't care, so I . . . sort of flirted with Zac. I dared him to take a drink, even put it in his Coke. He probably didn't turn me down just so my feelings wouldn't be hurt. I think he'd gotten the drift of what was going on between Scott and me—or what *wasn't* going on. . . ." Her voice trailed off. "So I kept refilling Zac's glass, and before we knew it . . ."

Her father's shoulders slumped even lower. But Mom and Jennifer were nodding encouragingly, so she went on. "I wanted Scott and Natalie to think I didn't care that they were together. But I was hurting really badly inside. So . . . I started drinking, too, just to numb the pain . . . you know? So you see, Daddy, I do understand." She turned to face him. He had his head in both hands. "Can you forgive me, Daddy?"

He didn't say a word, just sat shaking his head.

Katlyn glanced from her mother to Jennifer, who looked as blank as she felt. Was this the way it would be? No answer? No solution? No . . . nothing?

Then her daddy began to speak, mumbling at first. "The question is, can I forgive myself?" He continued to finger the glass, turning it this way and that so the liquid at the bottom was reflecting the light over the bar. "I haven't been a very good role model . . . putting adult things in the hands of children . . . expecting them to handle their lives more responsibly than I have." He looked up at Katlyn, his hair stringing over his eyes. "Sure, baby," he said, his voice breaking. "I forgive you . . . if you can forgive me."

"Oh, Daddy, don't do that." Katlyn reached out to touch the tear that rolled down his cheek. "I didn't mean to make you feel guilty. I just didn't want you to be so angry."

Her mother moved over to her father's side. "Do you realize what our Katlyn has done today?" she asked quietly, reaching over to tap the little dove with a delicate finger. "Do you know, Chan?"

"Yeah." He ran his fingers through his hair once more, then his hand moved forward, across the bar.

Katlyn wheeled around. She figured her parents needed some time alone. Jennifer followed close behind.

"Did I make things worse, Jen?" Katlyn asked after they had left the room, closing the door softly behind them.

"You did the right thing, Katlyn. Dad will have to make his own decisions . . . deal with his own feelings."

Katlyn nodded sadly. "I just wonder if he was reaching for another drink—or the dove?"

Thirteen

Natalie was elated when Scott showed up early for their date. They'd decided to go to a movie to get their minds off Zac's and Katlyn's troubles for a while. But the minute she was buckled into the front seat of his cranberry sports car, everything changed.

"Nat, I hope you don't mind, but Mr. Chander called a while ago. He wants all of us—our family, Cissy and her parents—over at their house tonight at eight. I have to be there." He shrugged apologetically. "You want to go with me?"

"Think there's going to be more yelling and screaming?" Natalie had had enough of that for one day. Apparently, peace and tranquility in the home was not something that just came with the territory. But she was beginning to realize just how lucky—no, blessed—she really was to have a family like hers.

"Dad said if anyone starts getting angry, we'll leave. Maybe Mr. Chander just wants to tell Zac off and get it off his chest, once and for all. I guess we're all prepared to listen to that, and Zac sure knows not to do anything that would violate his parole. He thinks it's a miracle the judge didn't sentence him with jail time!"

Natalie didn't want to get into the middle of a family feud. But if she didn't go, Scott would go without her, and he might need a friend tonight more than ever. Straightening her shoulders, she took a deep breath and lifted her chin. "I'm with you. Lead on."

He gave her one of those knee-weakening grins and turned the key in the ignition. The engine started up and purred like a kitten as they wound through the tree-lined streets. It was great that Zac didn't have to go to jail. But his sentence obviously hadn't satisfied the Chanders. Who was right? Natalie couldn't help but wonder if the sentence would have been the same if Zac had come from a poorer family instead of one of the most prominent families in town.

"You know, it seems like a miracle that Zac's not going to jail," Scott began, echoing her thoughts, "but if you stop and think about it, he's not really free. He may even have to drop out of college since he has to do community service and work to make payments to Katlyn. The legal papers won't allow Dad to pay it for him. And with a conviction on his record, he'd have trouble getting into med school anyway."

Natalie nodded. "He'll probably hate not being able to drive the most. You know how he loved that car." She thought of the fire-engine red Corvette that had ended up in a pile of twisted metal and shattered glass.

Scott glanced over at her. "He may find out who his *real* friends are."

"And dates. What about dates? Where can you take

a girl without a car these days?"

Scott was sober. "This will certainly test what he's made of . . . just like I've been tested . . . and not too long ago, as I recall." He gave a little laugh and turned onto the street where the Chanders lived.

Tonight may be one of those tests, Natalie thought, adding a prayer that Mr. Chander wouldn't lose his temper and commit *murder* right before their eyes!

When everyone was accounted for—Cissy and her mom and dad from next door; the four Lamberts, along with Aunt Martha; and the four Chanders, Katlyn, conspicuous in her wheelchair—Mrs. Chander invited them into the great room. Although the room was huge and there was plenty of seating, Natalie felt a little claustrophobic. Nerves, probably. As she glanced around, she couldn't help thinking that the twelve of them made up a full jury. Zac didn't count of course. He was the one who was on trial here. And as far as Mr. Chander was concerned, at least, the jury was still out!

The atmosphere was really tense. Natalie didn't know how to greet her friends, so she just nodded and smiled a kind of tight-lipped smile, then tried to melt into the sofa beside Scott. She'd know soon if she'd made the right decision to tag along.

Zac hung back until the last minute, then stepped into the room just as Mr. Chander stood up. There was instant silence. No one said a word. Zac wondered if anyone could hear the drumming of his heart. It was going ninety miles an hour!

Mr. Chander cleared his throat and gazed at the immaculate white carpet like there was a speck on it that ought to be removed or something. *He's probably thinking of me!* Zac controlled a shiver.

"This thing has been settled by the courts. But it hasn't been settled in *my* mind."

So far, no surprises. This was about what Zac had expected. But he couldn't help wondering if this was the place where Chander drew his gun and took aim.

Instead, the man squared his shoulders, took a deep breath, and continued. "This morning, I heard a lot of people accepting the blame for what Zac did. In my view, having been reared in a family with high moral standards, the boy knows right from wrong"—he glanced over at Helen Lambert—"in spite of your . . . problem, Helen. As a matter of fact, I admire you for your courage in taking the stand you took today." His gaze swiveled back to Zac. "But the ultimate guilt lies with this young man."

After a brief pause, he said, "*My* children are responsible for their actions, too. But there is a major difference here. On the night of the accident that injured my daughter, my wife and I left them at the lake house, knowing there was a party going on. Even with a minor in the house, we've always had"—he gestured toward the bar—"all that." Mr. Chander seemed to be fumbling for words. "We . . . *I* . . . put temptation in their path."

He scuffed his shoe on the carpet, then continued. "To be honest, Gina has mentioned more than once that we should turn our bar into a juice bar—some-

thing healthy for the girls and their friends. I ridiculed
the idea. What would *my* banking friends think? Most
of them—as I have been—are accustomed to a two-
martini lunch and a relaxing drink before dinner."
Again he looked down, then stuck his hand into the
pocket of his trousers and brought out a tiny object.

"Earlier this evening, Katlyn laid this little dove beside my shot glass. Somehow I knew it was a moment
of decision for me. If I reached for that glass, I'd just
try to drown all this bitterness inside of me."

Everyone stared at him, not believing what they
were hearing. He shook his head. "I'm through with it
. . . just as you are, Helen. With the help of God and
. . . my friends . . . I want to get rid of it."

Zac hadn't closed his mouth since Mr. Chander's
first statement. But there was more.

"Today I learned that the liquor that caused this
whole mess came from *my* bar in *my* house. It was tol-
erated by my eldest daughter"—he searched the faces
for Jennifer's solemn one, then swept the others until
his gaze came to rest on Katlyn—"and was offered to
him by my younger daughter."

Katlyn dropped her head, her cheeks flushing a
bright crimson. Zac felt sorry for her. He knew that
feeling. He jumped to his feet. "Excuse me, sir, but
she's only sixteen. I'm almost twenty. Don't blame *her*
for this."

Mr. Chander stared at him—man to man, eye to
eye. "There is something about Zac Lambert that occurred to me late this afternoon. I feel compelled to
mention it."

The tension in the room mounted. With one wrong

word, things could get out of hand and tempers would flare. "To my knowledge, Zac never once revealed that he was drinking my alcohol, with my daughters, at my house. He even refused to respond to the judge's direct order to cite the source of his alcohol. That refusal could have resulted in a contempt charge and a stiffer sentence." He drew a deep breath. "That does not exonerate him of all guilt, of course, but it does show a strength of character I must admit I find . . . very admirable." He studied the carpet for a long moment.

Zac was speechless. Mr. Chander lifted his head and looked him straight in the eye again. "But I'm not blaming my daughters, son, or even *you.* I'm blaming myself. Alcohol has destroyed a friendship my wife and I enjoyed with your parents. It's destroyed a friendship between our children. It's caused your family unfathomable grief. But more than that—I've never been so bitter and angry in my life. I was almost consumed by it . . . wanted to strangle you with my bare hands."

Zac squirmed at the thought of Mr. Chander's fingers around his throat.

"Gina has been encouraging me to do this for some time, but I wouldn't listen to her. I'm saying it now." He swallowed hard before going on. "I'm asking all of you to forgive me, though it may be very difficult . . . you, Elizabeth and John, Cissy; you, Lawrence and Helen . . ."

"No, Chan!" Zac's dad stood to interrupt him. "It isn't difficult at all. I can't blame you for having hard feelings toward my son. I've wanted to strangle Zac myself!"

Zac gasped, his mind reeling. Did the action start

now—with his own father? Or was it all over?

The grins and good-natured back-slapping and laughter told him his troubles were behind him.

"How about some refreshments?" Gina Chander was asking. "Lemonade and cookies."

"Sounds perfect to me!" Helen agreed, following her hostess into the dining room.

Zac waited until the adults had filed out of the room, chatting comfortably now that the ice was broken. That left the younger people still sitting there like lumps, looking at one another. What next?

"Let's go out on the patio," Jennifer suggested, holding the door while Katlyn wheeled herself out. She wiggled her finger at Zac. "You too."

A little self-conscious still, Zac stood and followed, pausing when he neared Mr. Chander, who was the last to leave the living room. Maybe the less said the better. But he had to say *something*. "Thank you, sir."

Mr. Chander only nodded, but there was a look of understanding in his eyes that hadn't been there before.

I've got a lot to prove to a lot of people, Zac thought as he joined the others on the patio. He wouldn't speak unless he was spoken to. Let them make the first move. He still felt a little like a criminal. Best for him to stay in the background and just wait it out.

Katlyn reached up to give Cissy a hug.

"You're looking terrific, Kat. You must have used some of those tips I gave you."

"Uh-huh. When are you going to New York?"

Cissy stepped back, shocked. "Did I say I was going?"

"You've *got* to go! You'll win. I just know it. Why wouldn't you—with that figure and that face?" She was teasing—like her old self—but she hoped Cissy could see the friendly twinkle in her eyes. *That* was new. It felt good—really good. "If you have time, send me a postcard and tell me all about it."

"You'll be the first!" Cissy promised.

"You look really pretty tonight, Katlyn," Scott said on his way to find a place near Natalie, who was already seated in a wicker chair.

Katlyn grinned at him. *Must be my insides showing*, she thought. *He never said that before, and I was in much better shape before the accident!*

"Thanks," she said, feeling something warm flowing through her. This was new, too—a new kind of love—for Scott, for everyone! Even for Natalie, who looked distinctly uncomfortable. Katlyn reminded herself not to gloat. Scott may have paid her a compliment, but he was *with* Natalie tonight. And it was okay. It was really okay.

"I'm so glad you're feeling better," Natalie spoke up.

"Me too." Katlyn smiled at her. "You don't know *how* glad."

A cooling breeze stirred the oak trees flanking the patio. In the distance, heat lightning lit the sky at intervals. Maybe it would rain and cool things off. And maybe that light flashing behind the dark clouds was a reminder of an adage she'd heard somewhere: *Every cloud has a silver lining.*

"Zac," she called to him, patting the chair next to her wheelchair. "Have a seat."

He stood for a moment, looking down at her. Slowly she raised her head and her eyes met his. She felt a little tingle she hadn't felt since the accident. His expression told her he felt it, too.

He dropped down beside her. "Hey, pretty lady," he said softly. "As you know, among *other* things"—he cleared his throat—"the judge sentenced me to community service. And the doctors have prescribed therapy for *you*. Since you're going to be spending a lot of time at the Rehab Center for the next few months, do you think you could stand a pretty regular dose of *me*?"

Natalie and Scott have been invited to go to New York City over the Thanksgiving holiday with Cissy, who will compete with ten finalists in the Great American Model Search. Will Cissy win? What will happen when Scott and Natalie finally spend time alone together in this magical, exciting place? Find out what surprises await them all in WHITE DOVE ROMANCE #4, *Picture Perfect*!

Teen Series From
Bethany House Publishers

Early Teen Fiction (11–14)

HIGH HURDLES by Lauraine Snelling
Show jumper DJ Randall strives to defy the odds and achieve her dream of winning Olympic Gold.

SUMMERHILL SECRETS by Beverly Lewis
Fun-loving Merry Hanson encounters mystery and excitement in Pennsylvania's Amish country.

THE TIME NAVIGATORS by Gilbert Morris
Travel back in time with Danny and Dixie as they explore unforgettable moments in history.

Young Adult Fiction (12 and up)

CEDAR RIVER DAYDREAMS by Judy Baer
Experience the challenges and excitement of high school life with Lexi Leighton and her friends—over one million books sold!

GOLDEN FILLY SERIES by Lauraine Snelling
Readers are in for an exhilarating ride as Tricia Evanston races to become the first female jockey to win the sought-after Triple Crown.

JENNIE MCGRADY MYSTERIES by Patricia Rushford
A contemporary Nancy Drew, Jennie McGrady's sleuthing talents promise to keep readers on the edge of their seats.

LIVE! FROM BRENTWOOD HIGH by Judy Baer
When eight teenagers invade the newsroom, the result is an action-packed teen-run news show exploring the love, laughter, and tears of high school life.

THE SPECTRUM CHRONICLES by Thomas Locke
Adventure and romance await readers in this fantasy series set in another place and time.

SPRINGSONG BOOKS by various authors
Compelling love stories and contemporary themes promise to capture the hearts of readers.

WHITE DOVE ROMANCES by Yvonne Lehman
Romance, suspense, and fast-paced action for teens committed to finding pure love.